# THE USBORNE
# COMPLETE BOOK OF DRAWING

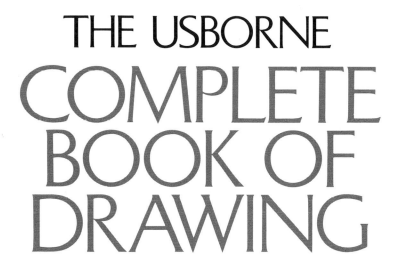

# THE USBORNE
# COMPLETE BOOK OF DRAWING

## Designed by Nigel Reece
## Edited by Alastair Smith and Judy Tatchell
### Additional designs by Fiona Brown

### Illustrated by
Victor Ambrus, Iain Ashman,
Terry Bave, Val Biro, Kim Blundell, Derick Bown,
Derek Brazell, Fiona Brown, Peter Bull, Chris Chapman, Kuo Kang Chen,
Peter Dennis, David Downton, Nicky Dupays, Rys Hajdul, Rosalind Hewitt,
Keith Hodgson, Philip Hood, Adam Hook, Chris Johnson, Colin King,
Kevin Lyles, Jamie Medlin, Paddy Mounter, Chris Reed, Peter Ross,
Graham Round, Jon Sayer, Peter Scanlan, John Shackell, Chris Smedley,
Guy Smith, Chris West, Claire Wright and Jo Wright

### Acknowledgments
Antique map of New York (page 107) courtesy of the British Library

Satellite image of Europe (page 105) courtesy of European Space
Agency/Science Photo Library

Photographs of Sydney Opera House (page 100) and Chrysler Building
(page 101) courtesy of the Image Bank

Photographs in PEOPLE section by Jane Munro Photography

The contents of this book are adapted from material previously published in the
Usborne How To Draw series, written by Pam Beasant, Moira Butterfield,
Marit Claridge, Janet Cook, Cheryl Evans, Emma Fischel,
Anita Ganeri, Alastair Smith, Lucy Smith and Judy Tatchell.

# Contents

First published in 1993 by Usborne Publishing Ltd, Usborne House, 83-85 Saffron Hill, London EC1N 8RT, England.
Copyright © Usborne Publishing Ltd, 1993.
The name Usborne and the device ⊕ are Trade Marks of Usborne Publishing Ltd.

# PEOPLE

People's bodies are made up of lots of different shapes so they are tricky to draw realistically. Don't try to draw a finished outline straight off. Instead, sketch rough shapes lightly and loosely until the proportions look right. Then you can start to refine the outline. In this section of the book, the rough shapes for many of the pictures are shown, to help get you started on the figure.

It is easier to draw people if you have a real person, or a photograph, to refer to. Keep looking at your model or photograph as you draw. The more closely you observe, the better your picture is likely to be.

Once you have mastered the technique of drawing cartoon people, also shown in this section, you can have fun experimenting with exaggerated expressions and movements. You can also find out how to draw caricatured likenesses of people.

# Heads and faces

Faces are the most expressive parts of people's bodies. They can be tricky to draw, but you can make them less difficult if you follow the steps shown on this page. Using pencil, start with an oval, then draw construction lines on it, as shown below.

**Draw the hair as a single shape, around the shape of the head. Keep the outline soft.**

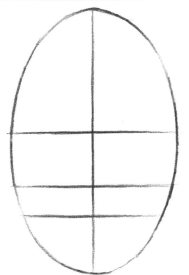

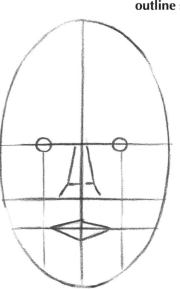

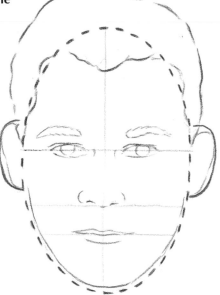

Draw a line just over halfway up the oval. The eyes and the bridge of the nose will go on this. The nose will end on the next line down and the mouth will run along the bottom line.

Sketch some rough shapes for the features using the lines as guides. Draw a line down from the middle of each eye. The corners of the mouth lie just within these lines.

Work on the shapes of the features, and sketch in the outline of the hair and ears. The tops of the ears are just above the eyes. Keep your pencil lines soft and light.

Shade thinly over the hair and face. Start to build up the shape of the face by adding further thin layers, especially in the areas which will be in shadow.

Leave the parts that catch the light with one or two thin layers on them. For shadowy areas, use several layers of shade. Add dark swirls to the hair to give it greater texture.

You can add darker shades to deepen the shadows on the face and hair. Make the darkest parts, such as the nostrils and parts of the hair, stand out by adding touches of black.

# Heads from different angles

These shapes show you how to vary the positions of the construction lines in order to draw heads from different angles. It is not easy to draw people's features realistically and position them correctly, but it does improve with practice. Try drawing people when they are likely to stay still for a long time, such as when they are reading or watching television.

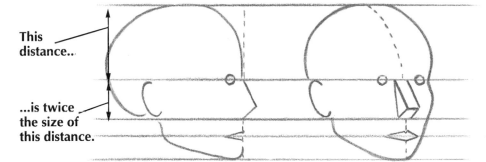

This distance...

...is twice the size of this distance.

**A drawing of the head done from the side is called a profile.**

**Three-quarter view. Curve the line down the middle of the face.**

# Drawing practice

For practice, you could fill a sheet of paper with close-up sketches of different features. It is easiest to copy them from life or from photographs. Don't colour them in - just concentrate on drawing the features and giving them shape. Leave the paper to show through for highlights and add shadows with a soft pencil. (You can find out about different kinds of pencils, and other materials, on pages 122-125.)

# Cameos

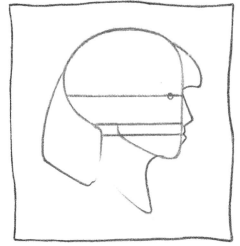

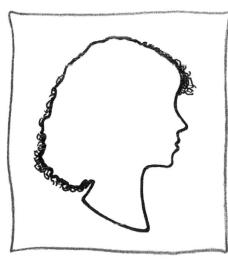

A cameo shows the silhouette of a head in profile. First, sketch the shape of the head and add construction lines in pencil. Then plot the shapes of the face and hair.

Refine the shapes of the face and hair until they are accurate. Draw over the outline with a fine ink pen, trying to keep the line smooth. Then erase any pencil sketch marks.

Finally, fill in the shape of the profile, using black paint or a felt tip pen. For the finished effect, cut out an oval shape around the silhouette.

7

# Cartoon faces

This page shows a quick way to draw a cartoon face. The technique uses a basic face shape with construction lines drawn on it to help with positioning the features. This technique is similar to the method used for drawing a real face, explained on the previous two pages. However, drawing a cartoon is much simpler than drawing a real face. Sketch the cartoon in pencil first.

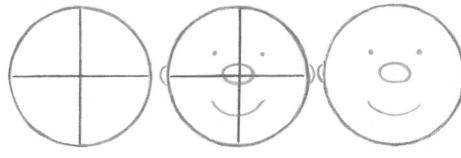

**Draw a circle with two faint pencil lines crossing it, dividing it into quarters.**

**Put the nose where the lines cross. The ears should be level with the nose.**

**Erase the lines crossing the face. You can now add hair, hats and expressions to the face.**

## Cartoons growing up

A baby's features are all in the lower half of the face.

Wisp of hair

High, round forehead

Toothy grin

Girls' and boys' faces are similar shapes but they can have different hairstyles.

More space between chin and mouth than on a baby.

To make a woman's face look rounder than a child's, space her eyes further apart.

Round eyebrows give a soft shape.

Many men have longer, more oval-shaped heads than women.

Straight, sloping eyebrows.

Make the nose bigger than on a child.

An old person's face is round, like a child's.

The hair grows far back on the head.

The ears are low down on the sides of the head.

Small eyes and sloping eyebrows.

# Different expressions

By varying the head shapes and altering the positions and shapes of features, you can create lots of different expressions for cartoon characters.

**Sly.** The eyes look sideways and the mouth is pursed.

**Winking.** The mouth tilts up on the side where the eye is closed.

**White stripes in the hair make it look shiny.**

**Smug.** Sideways grin and half-closed eyes.

**Angry.** The brow is creased and the mouth is tightly closed.

**Bored.** The mouth is a wavy line and the eyebrows are drooped.

**Wavy hair complements the shape of the mouth.**

**Yawning.** The nose squashes up to the eyes, which are closed. The mouth is wide open, showing the teeth and tongue.

**Sickly.** The face has a greenish tinge. The tongue hangs out. The eyes are creased.

**Deep in thought.** The eyes look up as if she is trying to picture something in her mind.

**Frightened.** The face is pale and bluish. Hair stands on end. Eyes are wide open.

# Drawing bodies

Begin your drawings of whole figures by making a sketch of the body, using pencil. Start your sketch by drawing the rough shapes of the main body parts, as shown on the right. Do the shapes shown in red first, then do the limb shapes shown in blue. When sketching, don't stop to erase mistakes, but carry on sketching lightly, improving the shapes as you sketch.

Check that the body parts are in proportion by seeing how many head-sized ovals make up the overall height. An adult man will probably be about seven heads tall. On average, women are about six and a half head-lengths tall. When the overall body shape looks correct, draw the outline of the clothes (shown in green on the right) around it.

Head

Shoulders

Chest

Stomach

Hips

**People in their mid-teens are about six head-lengths.**

**Four year olds are about three and a half head-lengths.**

**Sketch the positions of folds and creases lightly, using pencil. Then put a pale layer of shading over each item of clothing, plus the skin.**

**Shadows form where folds dip in. Highlights form where folds catch the light.**

**Highlights and shadows are usually curved, because they form around the body.**

**Shading areas of the body which curve away from you, such as the sides of the girl's sweater, can help to make a body look rounded.**

**Imagine where the light is coming from, and leave highlights on the areas that it will hit.**

**Add dark lines and patches to complete the darkest shadows. This will make the figures look solid.**

# Checking proportions

When drawing a live subject, you can use head-lengths to check their proportions. Shut one eye, then measure your subject's head with a pencil held at arm's length, as shown.

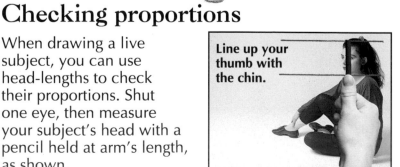

**Line up your thumb with the chin.**

Use the head measurement to see how many head-lengths make up the rest of the body, as in this picture.

# Cartoon bodies

You can start a cartoon by sketching a stick figure. Draw the outline of the figure around the sticks. Go over the completed outline with a black ink pen. Then erase the stick figure and colour the cartoon.

Erase part of the head line where the hair falls forwards.

The clothes' shapes are very simple.

In proportion to the body, the head is larger than on a real person.

Use bright felt tips to complete your cartoon.

The feet usually turn out.

Curves on the clothes show the rounded shape of the body.

When someone is facing you, you can see their thumbs and first fingers.

Leave a small, white patch on the shoes to make them look shiny.

# Walking and running

In a cartoon, you can exaggerate body positions to emphasize movements. Plan your drawings with stick shapes if it helps.

A walking person leans forwards slightly and always has one foot on the ground. The right arm is in front when the left leg is forward.

Starting to run, the body leans further forwards and the elbows bend.

Draw a running figure with the feet just off the ground.

The faster a person runs, the more the body leans forwards and the further the arms stretch.

Add a few curved lines to show fast movement.

# Jumping

Running towards the jump...

Taking off...

In mid-flight...

Landing from the jump.

This leg bends to push the body off the ground.

The legs stretch wide apart.

Both feet come forwards to hit the ground.

# People in action

It is helpful to get someone to pose for you while you draw. Even if you are drawing an action picture, you can sometimes get a model to fake the body position and keep still while you draw. There is an example of this below. The model lay on the floor with his feet close to the illustrator. This gave the illustrator the chance to copy the body shapes accurately. The picture was then completed by copying clothes and equipment from a photograph of a parachutist.

**Always make sure that your models are in a comfortable position when you draw them.**

**Bright clothing helps to make the picture look exciting.**

**To make the body look as if it is coming towards you, the shading becomes stronger and more detailed as it gets closer to you.**

**You could include the parachute canopy in the background.**

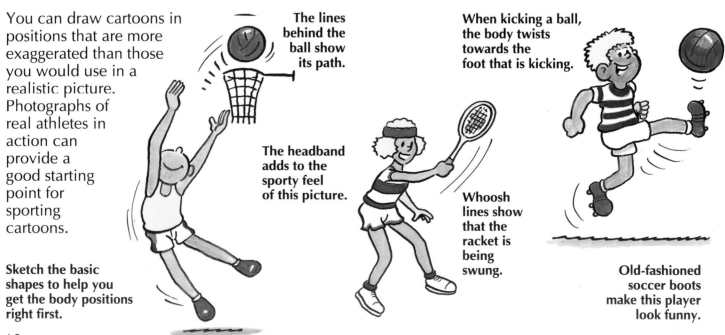

The angle of this picture makes the feet look as if they are bigger than the head. The body and legs look as if they are squashed. This kind of distortion is known as foreshortening. There is more about foreshortening on page 121.

## Cartoons in action

You can draw cartoons in positions that are more exaggerated than those you would use in a realistic picture. Photographs of real athletes in action can provide a good starting point for sporting cartoons.

**Sketch the basic shapes to help you get the body positions right first.**

**The lines behind the ball show its path.**

**The headband adds to the sporty feel of this picture.**

**When kicking a ball, the body twists towards the foot that is kicking.**

**Whoosh lines show that the racket is being swung.**

**Old-fashioned soccer boots make this player look funny.**

12

# High-speed skier

This skier has been drawn in a style which emphasizes the speed at which she is moving. Her extreme position, combined with the streaky shading, conveys danger and excitement.

**Begin by shading the lines far apart, as shown here. Leave highlighted areas with very few lines.**

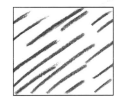

**Build up the darker areas by drawing the lines closer together, leaving less white space between them.**

**Add darker shades over light ones to create shadow. Areas of light and dark make the body look solid.**

Colours are sometimes described as cold or warm. For example, blues and greys are associated with cold things, such as steel or the sea. Oranges, yellows and reds are associated with warm things, such as fire and the Sun. In this picture, the warm-coloured figure stands out against the cool background.

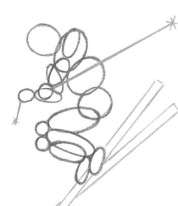

**If you want to copy this picture, start with the rough shapes shown here.**

**This picture mimics the effect that some sports photographers achieve, where a fast-moving image looks blurred and leaves a bright trail behind.**

**To help the figure stand out, shade the background to contrast with the figure's clothing.**

**Erase the rough shapes that will be covered by other body parts before you shade the picture.**

# Cartoon stereotypes

Stereotypes exaggerate certain things associated with different types of people. Many cartoons are stereotypes, or contain stereotyped features. They are not drawings of real people, but you can recognize from the pictures what sort of people they are or what they do for a living. Here are some examples.

A ballerina is very slim and light on her feet. She dances on the tips of her toes.

Emphasize her long limbs and slender waist.

Her frilled costume is called a tutu.

These lines show she is pirouetting.

A real burglar would never wear this kind of outfit but this is how they are often shown in cartoons.

Stolen property is carried in a swag bag.

The burglar creeps along on tip-toes.

A pop star wears loud, trendy clothes and eye-catching bangles and beads. Draw her making a big, excited gesture and with lights shining behind her.

Because of the loose style of the cartoon, the lights can be indicated in a very loose, quickly drawn way.

A spy's hat is pulled down and the collar of his coat is turned up. One furtive eye looks out from under the brim of his hat.

A hand in a pocket suggests that the spy is concealing something. Perhaps it is a top secret document.

A gangster wears smart clothes, smokes a cigar and carries a violin case with a gun hidden inside.

Dark glasses, to conceal the gangster's true identity.

14

# More cartoon people

Any person or situation can be turned into a cartoon, as shown by the examples on this page. You could use these characters in your comic strips. (There is a guide to creating these on page 21.)

A cartoon baby has a large head, a round backside and short limbs. Give it a toothy grin and a wisp of hair.

A crying baby bawls at the top of its voice. Exaggerate the size of the mouth.

The head is about one third of the total length of the body.

Babies sit with their legs straight out.

Short, fat limbs.

Children's heads are fairly large in proportion to the rest of their bodies.

Girls and boys are similar in size and height but they usually have different hairstyles.

Old people tend to be bent over. Their heads are placed further forward on their bodies than on younger people.

An old man's body is angular.

An old woman's body is more rounded than an old man's.

Make people look older by giving them spectacles or a walking stick.

# Cartoon effects

This person's legs look like they are spinning around. This and other effects give the impression that he is moving very fast.

You can write a word which symbolizes speed on the picture. *

Hair streams out behind.

Beads of perspiration

Movement lines

Clenched fists

Blurred colours show that the legs are moving rapidly.

Clouds of dust

Here, dashes of brown denote the shoes.

ZOOM!

Curved ground gives a sense of distance covered.

* See page 114 for more about lettering in cartoons.

# Colouring styles

The drawing and colouring style that you choose for a picture will affect its mood. Before you begin a drawing, decide on a style of drawing and colouring which will suit the atmosphere of the picture you want to show.

This jazz trumpet player is wearing a 1940s baggy suit. The drawing style emphasizes the size and shape of his suit, while the shading suggests the lighting and atmosphere of a dimly lit jazz club.

**Sketch the body shapes and the clothes in pencil. The position of the body makes a smooth curve from the head to the feet.**

**Draw lines where the clothes fold. You don't need to draw every small crease - just show the most obvious lines in the clothing.**

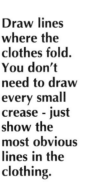

**Use the fold lines to help you divide your drawing into areas to be completed in different shades. Keep the shapes of these areas simple.**

Felt tips were used for this picture, to give it a bold feel. Only three shades of blue were used, and the shading was simplified into angular blocks of colour, to give the picture a stylized look. The main blocks are large, to stop the picture from looking fussy.

## Private eye

To paint a person looking like a private eye from an old movie, use black and light grey watercolours. To help you sketch the shadows, ask somebody to pose as a model for you. In a darkened room, shine a light on him or her from the side. Make sure that the model's head is tilted forwards slightly, to create a threatening appearance.

**Strong light should hit one side of the face, with no light on the other side.**

Sketch the figure, marking in the edges of areas of shade. Paint these areas grey. When dry, paint darker areas, such as on the hair and forehead, with a darker grey. To finish, paint the darkest areas black.

**To make shadows very dark, mix your black paint with hardly any water.**

**A coat with a turned-up collar gives the person a suspicious look.**

16

# Collage style

In a collage, pieces of coloured paper are cut out and stuck down instead of using paint or coloured pencils. To begin a collage, make a sketch of somebody, from life or from a photo. An eye-catching position, where the body makes a strong shape, will help to make the picture look interesting.

**The length of the body in relation to the head has been exaggerated a little, to give a "larger-than-life" feel.**

**Add simplified clothes shapes over your sketch.**

Trace the clothes shapes on to the pieces of paper. Cut out the tracings, using straight cuts and simplifying the shapes as far as possible. Glue the pieces on fresh paper. You can move the pieces slightly in relation to each other. This will make the picture look lively and impressionistic.

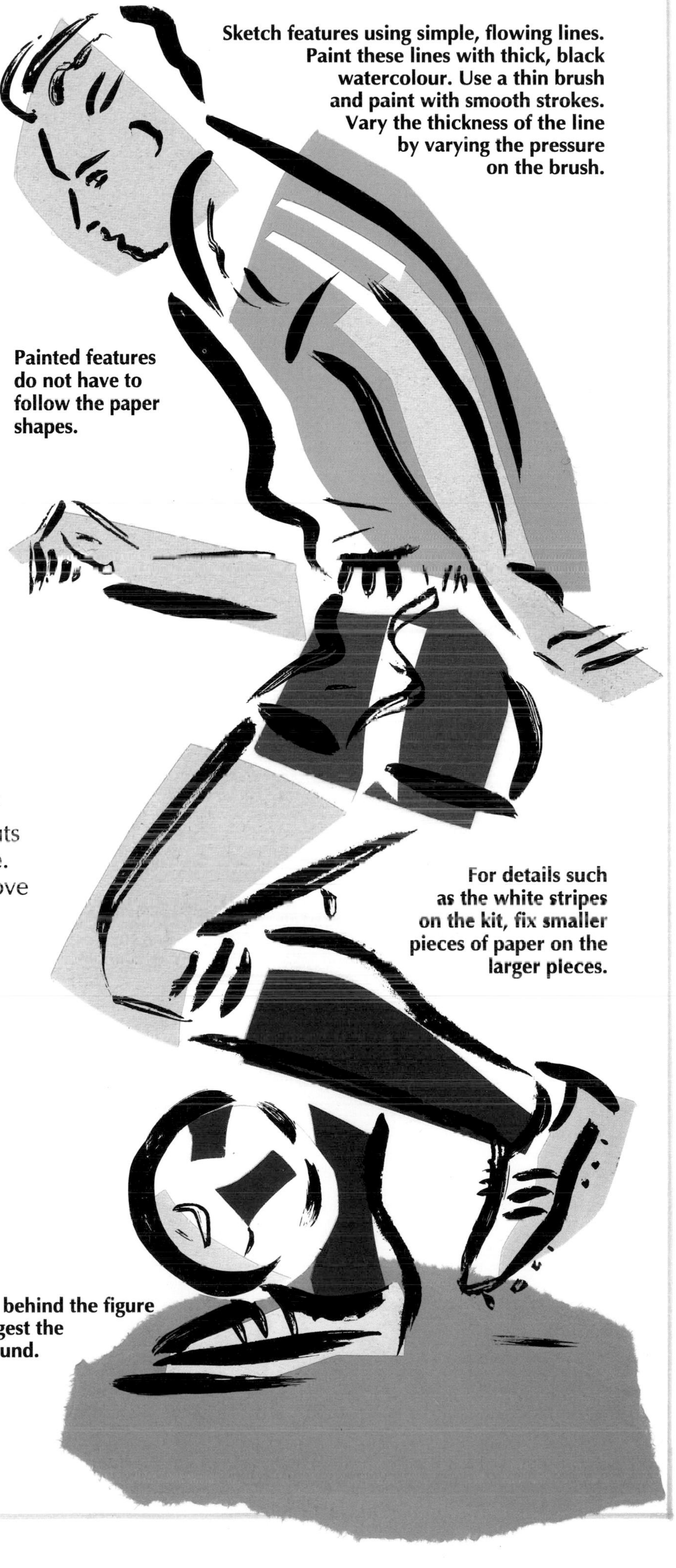

**Sketch features using simple, flowing lines. Paint these lines with thick, black watercolour. Use a thin brush and paint with smooth strokes. Vary the thickness of the line by varying the pressure on the brush.**

**Painted features do not have to follow the paper shapes.**

**For details such as the white stripes on the kit, fix smaller pieces of paper on the larger pieces.**

**Compare the shapes and positions of the shirt, shorts and leg shapes with the sketched shapes in the picture above.**

**A patch behind the figure can suggest the background.**

# Exaggerating body shapes

Illustrators often exaggerate the shapes and proportions of bodies, so that their drawings look more impressive and interesting. For example, fashion illustrators exaggerate people's shapes in order to emphasize the elegance of the clothes that they are wearing. To copy this fashion illustration, or to draw one like it, start by following the steps below.

**First, do a sketch of a posing model's body shapes. You can base the sketch on a photo of a real fashion model.**

**To make the figure look more elegant, sketch it with longer limbs. Make the whole body unnaturally long and slender.**

**Draw the simplified outlines of clothes over the body sketch. Keep the outline sleek and flowing.**

**For this painting style, use watercolours.**

**Paint the lightest tones, such as the skin tones, first. For very soft skin tones, mix your paint with a lot of water.**

**To make the clothes vivid, use only a little water to mix your paint. Use bold brushstrokes and do not show close detail.**

**You might like to design clothes of your own and show them on models drawn in this style.**

**Add dark swirls to the hair to give it texture.**

**Draw close details like the face and earrings last. Sketch them in pencil and then draw over them with an ink pen.**

**When the clothes and skin tones have dried, add dark, flowing outlines to enhance the graceful lines of the picture. Paint the outlines with single brushstrokes.**

**Exaggerate highlights by leaving large areas of white, as shown by the large streak that flows down the left leg.**

**Paint shadowy areas, such as the knees, using slightly darker tones. Show a minimum of detail.**

# Superheroes

Superheroes' muscles are exaggerated, to make them look like super-fit body builders. To make them look more gigantic and unreal, male superheroes' bodies are about nine head-lengths long, instead of the usual seven.

Superheroes have abilities that ordinary humans cannot match. For example, Spider-Man can climb anything and spin enormous webs. Often, he uses his webs to trap criminals.

You could make up your own superheroes, and design costumes for them. Draw them in athletic poses. For the most vivid effects use bright felt tip pens to decorate the costumes.

## Comparing proportions

The picture below shows what a superhero looks like when compared with an ordinary person. The size of the superhero's head is not exaggerated, but the body is much taller and broader than the ordinary person's.

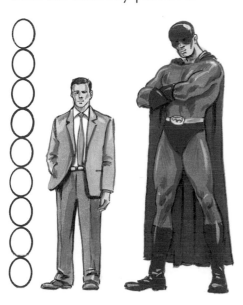

The features are outlined and shadows are shown using an ink pen.

Many superheroes hide their true identities beneath masks. Most wear a tight-fitting costume when they perform their heroics.

Sue Richards is a member of a crime-fighting group called the Fantastic Four. She has the power to disappear, so she is known as the Invisible Girl.

Comic strip figures are usually finished in a flat, bright style.

Female superheroes are extremely athletic, but not as musclebound as their male counterparts.

Superheroes at rest often stand in dramatic, domineering poses like this.

The colour fades from bottom to top as the Invisible Girl disappears.

19

# Caricatures

Caricatures deliberately overstate a person's features to make them look funny. The best caricatures also manage to highlight the subject's personality.

Before you start drawing, imagine the person that you want to caricature. Remember which of their features make the strongest impression in your mind. Make those features the most obvious ones in your caricature.

Features such as the glasses, bushy hair, big boots and a confident stance make the subject in this photo ideal for turning into a caricature.

Start your caricature by tracing or copying a photograph of the subject, in pencil. Without using any detail, show the important features.

Once you have done a simplified drawing, decide how to alter your subject. For example, you might want to make the legs skinnier and the boots bigger.

**To enlarge a feature, trace slightly outside the lines of the previous drawing.**

**To shrink a feature, trace slightly inside the lines of the previous drawing.**

**After several stages of tracing, the drawing should have altered drastically.**

**Make sure that the original person can be recognized in the caricature.**

Make several new tracings, exaggerating the features a little more with every new tracing.

When the figure has been exaggerated enough, do a final drawing and go over the outline with an ink pen.

Complete the picture using bright felt tips, as you would if you were drawing a cartoon character.

20

# Comic strips

The story below shows many of the important elements in a comic strip. One of the hardest things about drawing a comic strip is making the characters look the same in each frame. Give them simple, strong features, so that they are easy to repeat.

The shape of a speech bubble can suggest the way something is said, or thought. For more about creating cartoon lettering, see page 114.

The speech bubble of the first speaker should be positioned above and to the left of the second speaker's speech bubble.

A jagged speech bubble suggests an ear-splitting noise.

Give characters exaggerated facial expressions and body positions.

Keep speech short so that speech bubbles do not take up much room.

Question marks and punctuation marks can be used to express a state of mind.

Place speech bubbles over unimportant background areas.

Use bright felt tips for the characters, to make them eye-catching.

## Famous comic strip characters

Here are three examples of famous comic strip drawings.

Tintin is a young reporter who cannot resist getting involved in solving mysterious crimes. Tintin stories are long and are drawn in great detail. Each story has about 800 frames.

Tintin's clothes are drawn in more detail than his face. His simple facial features make him look honest and friendly.

Asterix is a warrior who lives in Gaul (part of ancient France). He and his friends are dedicated to protecting Gaul from their enemies, the Roman army.

Helmet and dagger show that Asterix is a warrior.

Large head, hands and feet make Asterix look cuddly.

Huge, rounded features look funny, not threatening.

Minnie the Minx appears in a weekly British comic, called *The Beano*. She is extremely cheeky, and likes to play tricks on people. She is usually brought to justice at the end of every story.

Messy hair shows that Minnie does not care about her appearance.

Big mouth, knobbly knees and wild expression emphasize Minnie's sense of humour.

Comic strips first appeared about a hundred years ago. The sort of style shown here is called "funnies" style. This is because it was first used in the USA, where comic strips in newspapers are called "funnies".

21

# Horror show

To make somebody look like a terrifying character from a horror movie, shine a light up from the floor, just in front of them, as shown in the photo below. This creates harsh, ghoulish shadows in the hollows of the face. In the painting at the bottom, the person in the picture has been transformed into a vampire. A made-up background has been added to show that she is stalking a graveyard late at night. The castle could be her grisly home.

**The light should shine brightly to make the shadows as sharp as possible. Do not let it shine directly into the eyes, though.**

To do a painting like this one, use watercolours. Apply the paint in layers, called washes, starting with the lightest shade. To create sharp edges, allow each layer of paint to dry completely before you apply another. To add details over watercolour (such as the trickle of blood and the highlights on the hair) use gouache or poster paints. These keep their true tones when used over watercolour.

**For shadowy streaks, such as on the hair, add thin stripes of darker watercolour over a still damp wash.**

**Shadows around the bottoms of the eyes and light just below the eyebrow make the eyes look weird.**

**The shape of the nose is altered by the harsh shadows formed on it.**

**A trickle of blood shows that the vampire has recently claimed a victim.**

## Spooky silhouettes

For extra spookiness, you could add a number of silhouettes to your vampire scene. Here are some suggestions, although you might like to invent some of your own.

**Bats are associated with vampires, although most bats are timid and completely harmless.**

**Bloodshot eyes give the impression that the vampire is in a trance.**

**The chin has little definition because it is so brightly lit.**

**For the background, use blues and greys to give the scene a moonlit quality.**

# ANIMALS

As well as a variety of shapes, animals have lots of different body coverings, from the smooth coat of a horse to the soft fur of a long-haired cat, or the shiny shell of a snail. There is help with showing these different textures, as well as drawing the animals' shapes, in this section.

You will find some animals easier to draw than others. It helps to draw while looking at a real animal, but the disadvantage of this is that most animals don't stay still for long. Instead, refer to a photograph, or if you have a pet, try drawing it while it is asleep.

Cartoon animals are easier to draw because the shapes are simplified. The challenge with a cartoon is to bring out the characteristics of the animal in an amusing way.

# Drawing cats

It helps to think of a cat as made up mostly of simple, rounded shapes. You can see this in the sketched drawing at the bottom of the page. Try to use smooth, curving lines to bring out its graceful build.

**The spine is long and very supple. The tail is really an extension of the spine, so try to make the two flow in a continuous line.**

**The head is quite small compared with the body.**

**The line of the cat's belly is almost straight.**

**Make the eyes yellowish green. Add darker green at the top and around the solid black pupils.**

**The legs join the body high up, not at tummy level.**

**Show the muscles with dark lines.**

**Shade the parts on which light does not fall directly, to give the cat form.**

Draw the main body shapes as shown on the right. Refine the outline and apply a pale grey-blue base. Let the paper show through on the lightest parts to give a sheen to the fur.

24

# A cat's eyes

The most striking things about a cat's face are its eyes. You can make the eyes look more alive, intense and realistic by simply making them darker at the top and lighter towards the bottom. A white highlight makes the eyes look bright.

**In strong light, the pupil closes up until it is just a narrow slit.**

**In good light, the pupil is a medium-sized oval, pointed at both ends.**

**In dim light, the pupil widens and is circular, filling most of the eye.**

# Drawing the head

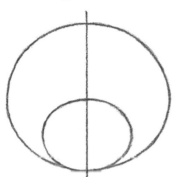

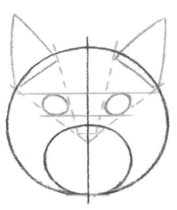

Draw two slightly flattened circles. A line down the middle will help you position features evenly on each side of the face.

Draw a little upside-down triangle for the nose. Lines radiating out from this will help you position the eyes and ears.

Soften the nose shape. Add the mouth as an upside-down Y-shape. Erase the sketch lines and apply a layer of pale fawn.

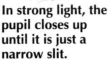

**The eyes and nose together form a V-shape.**

**The skull is fairly broad and rounded on top.**

**The eyes are spheres so the highlight falls in the same place on each eye.**

**Shading along the outer edge makes the ears look three-dimensional.**

**Draw the whiskers last, in white. Do little dots where each whisker grows.**

**Shade under and around the muzzle to bring it out from the face.**

# Cats in action

Cats are very agile, so drawing them in action is hard because they move fast and get into all sorts of acrobatic positions. Start with some simple line sketches. If the picture looks too static, like the one on the right, abandon it and try again.

Keep sketching until your lines start to flow. Exaggerating them a bit, as in the picture on the right, can improve the sense of movement.

Once the basic lines are right, put in the body shapes as shown. Use a soft pencil and don't press hard at this stage: keep the lines light and flowing.

Improve the outlines, making them stronger and cleaner. Erase any unwanted marks before applying a fawn base. Add a second layer to the undersides. Complete the cat by adding russet stripes as in the picture below.

**The position of the legs makes this sketch look too static.**

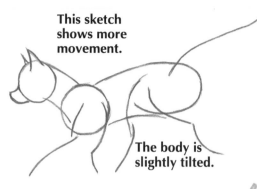

**This sketch shows more movement.**

**The body is slightly tilted.**

**Lifted paws show that the cat is in midstride.**

## Drawing fur

For short fur, start with a layer of the palest colour. If using watercolour, let this coat dry. Then add short, close, darker strokes.

For longer fur, use longer, looser strokes of colour. Group several strokes together, as shown, for a tufted effect.

Rex cats have tightly curled fur. Do rows of short, arched strokes close together over a base layer. Let this show through in between the rows.

**Keep the outlines soft. A hard outline will make the picture look flat and unrealistic.**

**The eyes fixed ahead give a purposeful look.**

**Apply individual hairs with a thin brush or very sharp coloured pencil, using short strokes. This will make the fur look realistic.**

**Showing stripes that are curving and stretching helps give a sense that the muscles are moving.**

**For the dark markings, apply broad stripes of watercolour.**

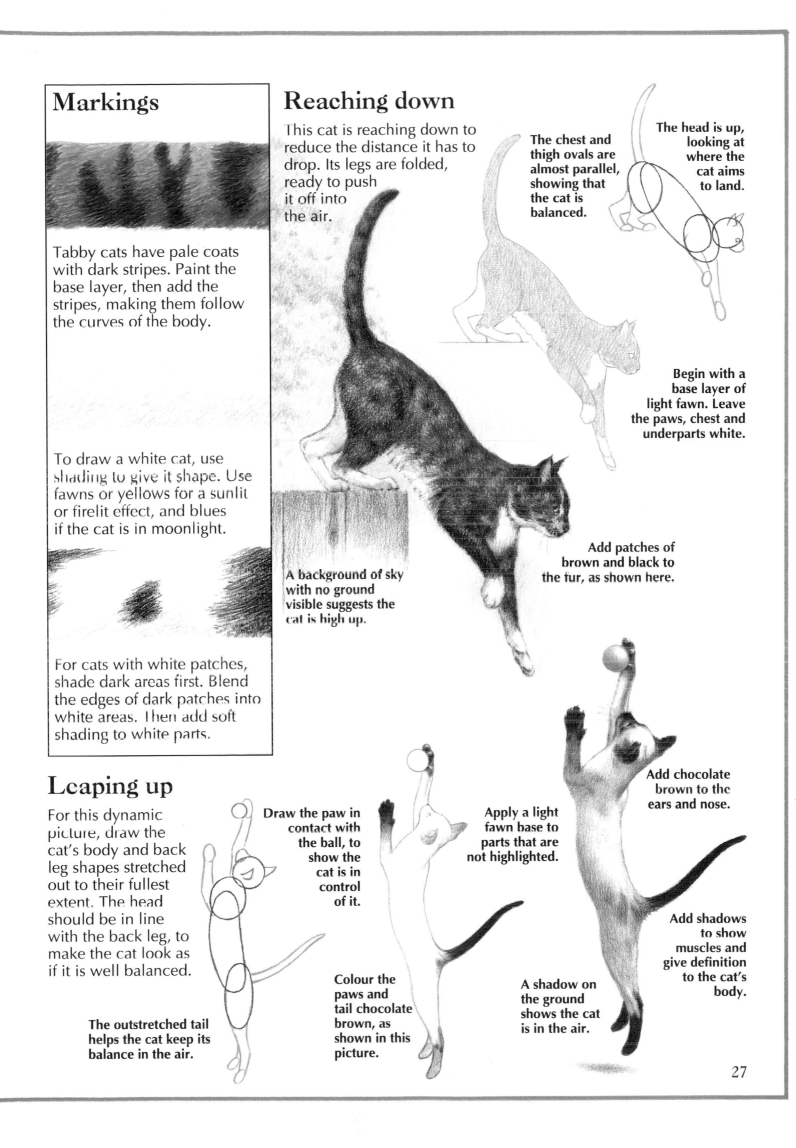

## Markings

Tabby cats have pale coats with dark stripes. Paint the base layer, then add the stripes, making them follow the curves of the body.

To draw a white cat, use shading to give it shape. Use fawns or yellows for a sunlit or firelit effect, and blues if the cat is in moonlight.

For cats with white patches, shade dark areas first. Blend the edges of dark patches into white areas. Then add soft shading to white parts.

## Reaching down

This cat is reaching down to reduce the distance it has to drop. Its legs are folded, ready to push it off into the air.

The chest and thigh ovals are almost parallel, showing that the cat is balanced.

The head is up, looking at where the cat aims to land.

Begin with a base layer of light fawn. Leave the paws, chest and underparts white.

Add patches of brown and black to the fur, as shown here.

A background of sky with no ground visible suggests the cat is high up.

## Leaping up

For this dynamic picture, draw the cat's body and back leg shapes stretched out to their fullest extent. The head should be in line with the back leg, to make the cat look as if it is well balanced.

The outstretched tail helps the cat keep its balance in the air.

Draw the paw in contact with the ball, to show the cat is in control of it.

Colour the paws and tail chocolate brown, as shown in this picture.

Apply a light fawn base to parts that are not highlighted.

Add chocolate brown to the ears and nose.

A shadow on the ground shows the cat is in the air.

Add shadows to show muscles and give definition to the cat's body.

# Kittens

Kittens' bodies are rounder than those of adult cats, and their heads are larger in relation to their bodies. Also, the distance between their front and back legs is shorter. Kittens are less co-ordinated than adults so they hold themselves differently, especially when they are very young, as this four-week-old kitten shows.

The lowered head and drooping whiskers give this kitten a sleepy, vulnerable look.

The kitten is shown leaning back on its back legs because it is so unsteady on its feet.

Short, pointed tail

Use short strokes for a soft look. A blurred outline looks furry.

A young kitten has a blunt muzzle.

The head shape is almost the same size as the chest.

The legs are short and thick, with big paws, in relation to the body.

## Kittens at play

Both of the kittens below look slightly off balance. This gives a feeling of movement to the picture. Draw the ginger kitten's body parallel with the black kitten's left foreleg.

The black kitten's body is foreshortened. For more about foreshortening, see page 121.

For an alert look, this kitten's ears are pointed forwards and the tail sticks up.

This picture was done with coloured pencils on grainy paper. This helps to give a soft look to the kittens' bodies.

## A cat and kittens

To draw this grouping, position the mother cat before starting on the kittens. Use different colours and markings for each of the kittens to add variety.

The broken lines show the layout of the picture. Space the kittens evenly between the cat's front and back legs.

The kittens' heads and bodies overlap. Their legs and paws are tucked away out of sight.

The cat's body is long and loose, while the kittens are rounded and tightly packed together.

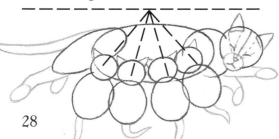

For a life-like touch, the kittens' tails are drawn in different positions.

Closed eyes give the cat a peaceful look.

# Cartoon cats

Before you draw a cartoon cat, plan which aspects of its looks and character you would like to show. This picture of kittens emphasizes their large heads and round bodies. It also shows that they love playing games.

**In the sketch, the shapes and features of a real cat are exaggerated.**

**Tiny movement lines add energy and action.**

**Real cats don't smile but you can add any expression you like to a cartoon cat.**

**For a tabby colour, use a light brown base with dark brown stripes.**

## Alley cat

Alley cats are rough and tough and will eat almost anything they can lay their paws on. They make excellent subjects for cartoons.

**Make the sketched shapes as simple as possible, to ensure that the final shapes are simple, too.**

**A nicked ear suggests the cat has been in a fight.**

**Around the outline, the occasional zigzag gives a scruffy look.**

**A big grin gives a jaunty air.**

**The whiskers are bent and ragged.**

**The fish skeleton shows that the cat has been scavenging.**

## Sly cat

This sly-looking Siamese cat is creeping along. Its long, low body and wavy tail illustrate its slinky movements. Its pointed, diamond-shaped face gives it a cunning air.

**The tail looks a little like a slithery snake.**

**The length of the body is exaggerated, to emphasize the sneaky quality of the cat.**

**The dark brown mask makes the cat look sinister.**

**Bright blue eyes look mesmerizing.**

**The cat has a creamy white body.**

**Light brown paws**

29

# Wild cats

With their dramatic markings and powerful, elegant bodies, wild cats can make striking drawings. Though they seem different from pet cats, in fact they have a similar body structure. You can turn them into cartoons by exaggerating their shapes and simplifying their markings.

## A tiger

The tiger is the biggest cat. It has lumpier shoulders, thicker legs and heavier paws than a pet cat. Its head is less rounded. As it walks, it holds its tail low, but curling upwards.

## A tiger's head

The head should be quite broad, with small, round ears and tufts of thick fur around the jaws.

**From the front, a tiger's muzzle is oval-shaped.**

## A cartoon tiger

**Exaggerate the furry jaws. This will make the tiger amusing even if it is in a bad mood.**

**The tiger's stubby legs emphasize its stocky power.**

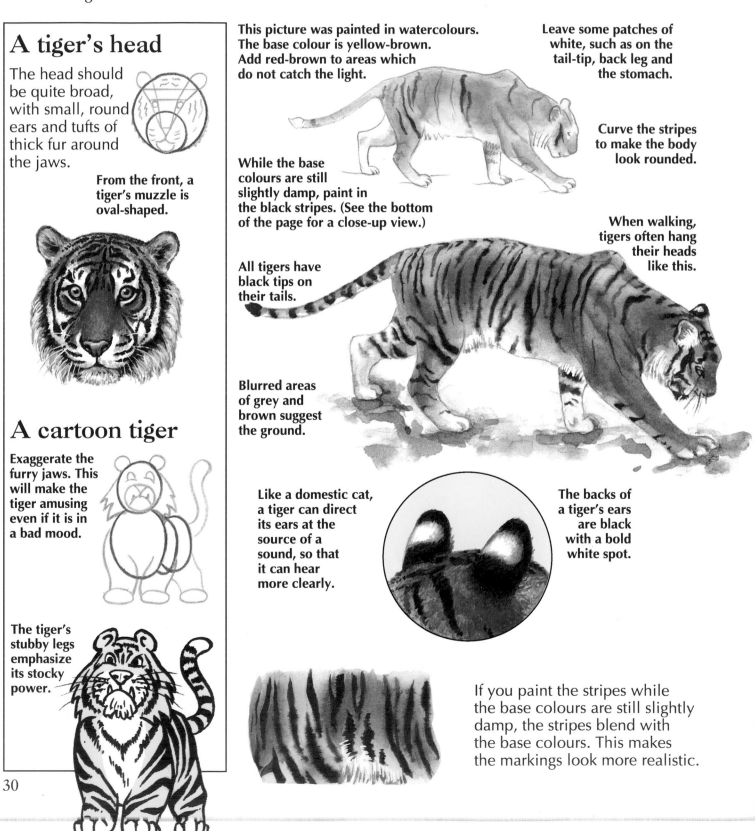

This picture was painted in watercolours. The base colour is yellow-brown. Add red-brown to areas which do not catch the light.

**While the base colours are still slightly damp, paint in the black stripes. (See the bottom of the page for a close-up view.)**

**All tigers have black tips on their tails.**

**Blurred areas of grey and brown suggest the ground.**

**Leave some patches of white, such as on the tail-tip, back leg and the stomach.**

**Curve the stripes to make the body look rounded.**

**When walking, tigers often hang their heads like this.**

**Like a domestic cat, a tiger can direct its ears at the source of a sound, so that it can hear more clearly.**

**The backs of a tiger's ears are black with a bold white spot.**

If you paint the stripes while the base colours are still slightly damp, the stripes blend with the base colours. This makes the markings look more realistic.

# A cheetah

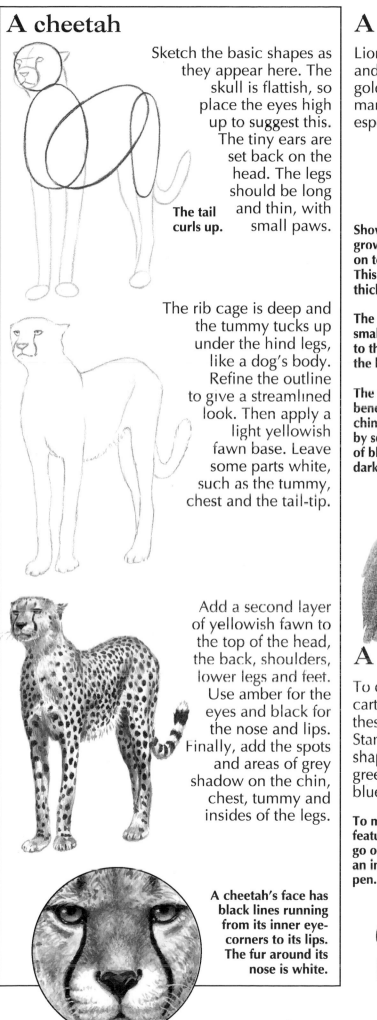

Sketch the basic shapes as they appear here. The skull is flattish, so place the eyes high up to suggest this. The tiny ears are set back on the head. The legs should be long and thin, with small paws.

**The tail curls up.**

The rib cage is deep and the tummy tucks up under the hind legs, like a dog's body. Refine the outline to give a streamlined look. Then apply a light yellowish fawn base. Leave some parts white, such as the tummy, chest and the tail-tip.

Add a second layer of yellowish fawn to the top of the head, the back, shoulders, lower legs and feet. Use amber for the eyes and black for the nose and lips. Finally, add the spots and areas of grey shadow on the chin, chest, tummy and insides of the legs.

**A cheetah's face has black lines running from its inner eye-corners to its lips. The fur around its nose is white.**

# A lion

Lions have long, heavy faces and chins. Only males have golden manes. Often, the mane looks ragged, especially on older lions.

**First, sketch an oval shape for the face, then add the facial features. Finally, sketch the mane.**

**Show the mane growing upwards on top of the head. This shows how thick it is.**

**The eyes are small in relation to the size of the head.**

**The thick fur beneath the chin is shown by squiggles of black and dark grey.**

**This close-up of a mane, in coloured pencil, shows how the colours are built up in red-brown and dark grey over a layer of pale gold.**

# A cartoon lion

To create a smug looking cartoon lion, follow these basic shapes. Start with the red shapes, then the green, then the blue.

**To make the outlines and features look striking, go over them with an ink pen.**

**A huge head makes the lion look silly.**

**Hooded eyes give this lion a superior expression.**

31

# Drawing a horse

Horses are some of the most beautiful animals to draw but also some of the most difficult because of the complicated nature of their body structure and proportions. In pencil, try copying the horse below by doing the shapes and lines shown in red first, then the green, then the blue.

**The top line of the neck forms a smooth curve. The lower line is shorter and straighter.**

**The head is made up of two ovals (see next page).**

**The outer edges of the buttock, hock and fetlock are in a straight line.**

**The circle for the chest is the same size as the circle for the hindquarters.**

**The hocks are set just a fraction higher than the knees on the front legs.**

Hocks

**The hindlegs join the body higher up than the forelegs and slope down and back to the hock joints.**

All the yellow lines on the sketch are the same length. You can use these lines to check that different parts of the horse are the correct size in relation to each other.

**The hooves can be done as box shapes.**

Fetlocks

**Highlights on the horse's hindquarters make them look rounded and glossy. To get this effect, let the pale base show through.**

**A long line of deep shading creates the dark crease down the underside of the neck, called the jugular groove.**

**Use a blend of long white, yellow and grey strokes for the tail.**

**Shadows on the undersides of the knees and fetlocks make them look rounded.**

When you are happy with the outline, apply a pale yellow-gold base. Gradually deepen the coat with layers of darker gold and brown. If using paint, as here, let each layer dry before applying the next.

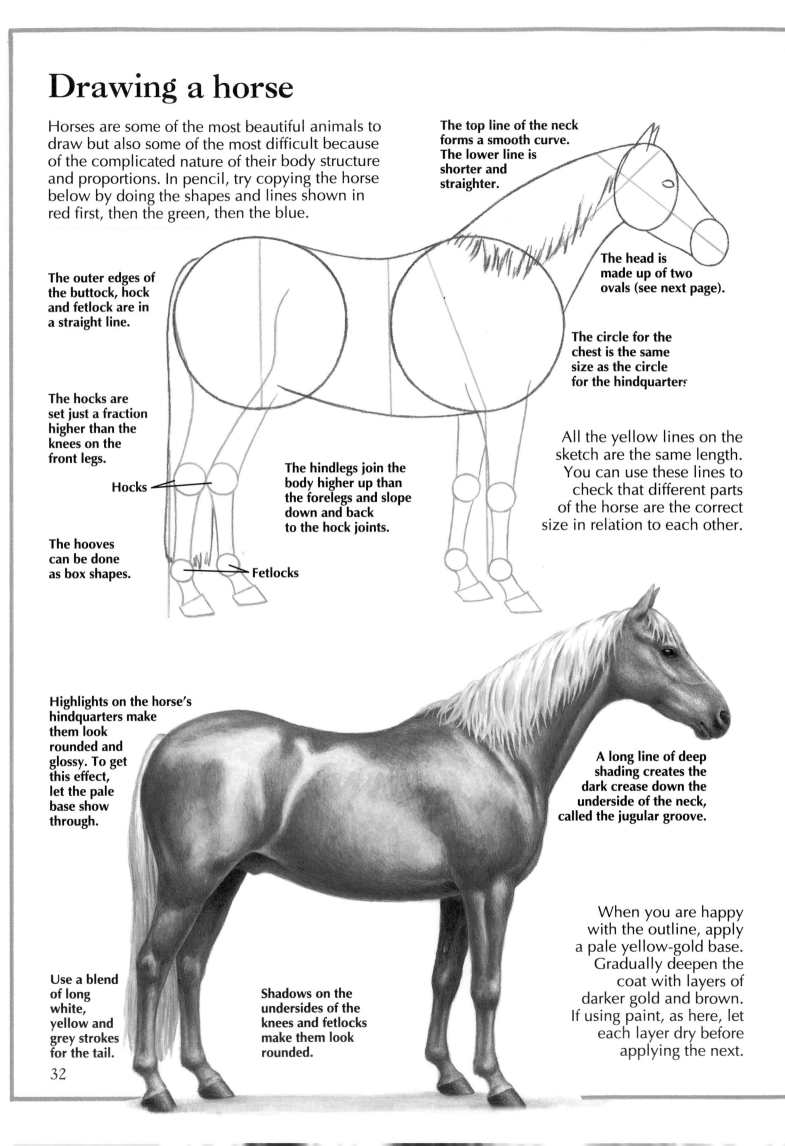

32

# A horse's head

Do a large, tilted oval for the main part of the head. Add a smaller overlapping oval, slightly more upright, for the muzzle. The green lines show the outlines of the neck and head.

Construction lines help to position the features.

This distance...

...is slightly shorter than this distance.

This is about half the distance above.

Refine and smooth off the outlines and erase the construction lines. Apply a thin coat of pale gold as the base. Let the paper show through on the lightest parts.

Add very fine, curved eyelashes.

Paint the eyes black and add a tiny white dot, or highlight, to give them shine.

Dark shadows inside the nostrils give them depth.

Soft brushstrokes give a velvety feel to the muzzle.

A lot of contrast between shadowy and highlighted areas shows off the shape of the horse's head.

This kind of horse, with a golden coat and white or flaxen mane and tail, is known as a palomino.

# Adapting the basic shapes

All horses' heads have the same basic structure, but the proportions may vary. For instance, the foal on the right has a leaner, less well-defined shape. On the far right, you can see how a bridle helps to frame a head. Curving the straps makes it look three-dimensional.

# The paces

Horses have four different paces, or gaits. A single moment from each of the gaits is illustrated on these pages. The pictures also show in sequence how colour can be built up, using coloured pencils.

**The neck is held long and relaxed.**

## Walk

This is a smooth gait in which the horse lifts and sets down each hoof in turn. First, sketch the shapes shown at the top of the page, in pencil. When the horse's proportions are correct, work on the outline until you have a finished sketch, like the one on the right.

**Before you begin shading, mark the positions of the eyes, nostrils, mane and mouth.**

**Erase any mistakes so that you can see the correct outline clearly.**

**The hooves flick up towards the back of the horse when they are lifted.**

## Trot

In this springy, two-time motion, opposite legs, known as diagonals, are moved at the same time. To begin colouring the horse, apply a smooth layer of the base colours, shown on this picture, over the whole body.

**The neck is arched.**

**The head is carried high, but held still.**

**Initially, make the shading very light on the tail, mane and legs.**

**Add a second layer of the base colour to areas that are in shadow.**

**The tail floats slightly to give a sense of movement.**

34

## Canter

This is a bounding, rocking, three-beat movement. The horse sets down one back hoof, then a pair of diagonals, then the last front hoof. Add reddish brown over the horse, letting the base colour show through on parts which catch the light.

**The mane bounces up and down.**

**The head is held high and swings as the horse moves.**

**The tail swishes up and from side to side.**

**Use reddish brown to show the shapes of the flexing muscles. These are most noticeable on the legs, neck, shoulders and hindquarters of a running horse.**

**Add a second layer of reddish brown to shadowy areas.**

**More strokes of grey give shape to the muzzle, mane, tail, lower legs and hooves.**

## Gallop

This is the fastest and most dramatic pace of all, in which the horse puts all of its effort into going as fast as it can.

**The neck and head are stretched forward.**

**The streaming mane and tail show that the horse is going extremely fast.**

**Thicken the mane and tail with strokes of black coloured pencil. Streaks of white coloured pencil on top prevent them from looking solid.**

**Add dark reddish brown to the undersides, under the muscles and along the back. Put a thin layer of black on parts that are in the darkest shadow.**

35

# Horses in action

Horses are lively and can be nervous. They may rear if startled or excited. A horse rearing high on its hindlegs makes a dramatic picture. The bottom half of this page shows how this piebald (black and white) horse was done in watercolours, starting with the small picture showing its basic shapes in red, green and blue.

**Paint the muzzle with a very light pinkish wash.**

**Only paint the parts of the horse which are in deep shadow solid black.**

**The mane and tail are the same colour as the parts of the body from which they grow.**

**Pinkish beige watercolour and grey pencil stripes give the hooves shape.**

**A vertical weightline through the hindquarters and hocks helps to make the horse look properly balanced.**

**Streaks of white pencil prevent the tail from looking solid.**

**The left foreleg is nearly at right angles to the weightline.**

Before painting the horse, mark in the edges of the piebald patches and sketch the eyes, nostrils and mouth.

Paint a layer of violet where the black patches will be. Dabs of pale grey start to give shape to the white areas.

Build up the darker shades. Let the white paper and the violet base layer show through on the highlighted parts of the coat.

# A jumping horse

This picture is very dramatic because of the angle from which it is drawn. The strong contrast between the dark and light areas also adds to its impact. A fairly hard, 3H pencil was used to shade the paler areas, while the eyes, jacket and boots were done in a softer HB.*

Look at the green construction lines shown below to see how the various parts of the horse and rider are positioned in relation to each other.

**The rider's knees are level with the top of the muzzle.**

**Leave the rear hooves with hardly any shading, to make them look further back.**

In the picture above, the three main ovals in the horse's body overlap and much of the body is hidden, because the horse is coming towards you.

Since the horse is coming towards you, the nearest hoof looks bigger than the hooves further away. This effect, where proportions are altered because of the angle from which the body is seen, is called foreshortening (see page 121).

*For more information about pencils, see page 122.*

# Show jumping

In a show jumping competition, a horse and its rider have to clear a course of jumps which can involve lots of twists and turns between obstacles. The course is a tough test of a horse's fitness and suppleness. The picture on the opposite page uses gouache for a powerful, dynamic effect. It is drawn from low down, as if the viewer is looking up at the horse. This increases the sense of height and makes the jump look impressive.

Follow the stages on this page to copy the picture, starting with the shapes on the right.

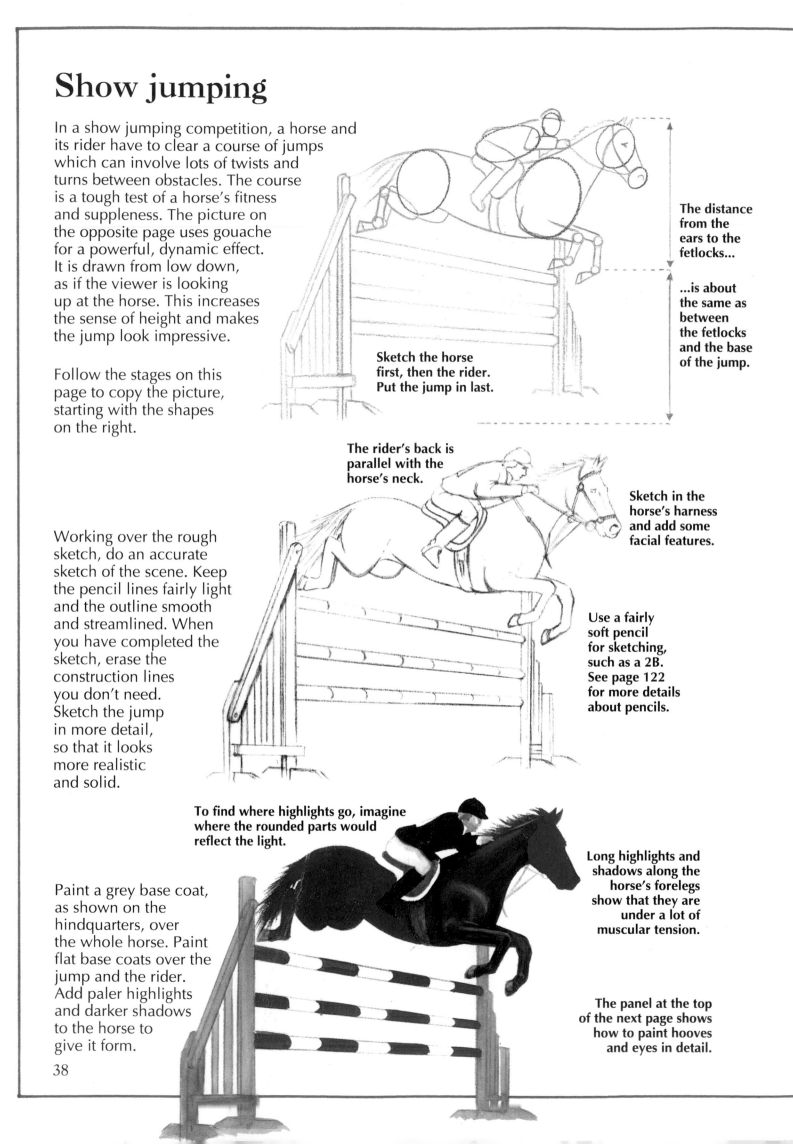

The distance from the ears to the fetlocks...

...is about the same as between the fetlocks and the base of the jump.

**Sketch the horse first, then the rider. Put the jump in last.**

**The rider's back is parallel with the horse's neck.**

**Sketch in the horse's harness and add some facial features.**

Working over the rough sketch, do an accurate sketch of the scene. Keep the pencil lines fairly light and the outline smooth and streamlined. When you have completed the sketch, erase the construction lines you don't need. Sketch the jump in more detail, so that it looks more realistic and solid.

**Use a fairly soft pencil for sketching, such as a 2B. See page 122 for more details about pencils.**

**To find where highlights go, imagine where the rounded parts would reflect the light.**

Paint a grey base coat, as shown on the hindquarters, over the whole horse. Paint flat base coats over the jump and the rider. Add paler highlights and darker shadows to the horse to give it form.

**Long highlights and shadows along the horse's forelegs show that they are under a lot of muscular tension.**

**The panel at the top of the next page shows how to paint hooves and eyes in detail.**

38

# Drawing details

### Hoof

Make the hoof mid-brownish grey. Add shading towards the front and back and along the top.

Soft dark and light stripes, very close together, show the bony texture of the horse's hoof.

### Eye

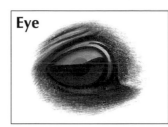

Draw the eye shape and sketch the lid above it. Make the eye black and the lid dark grey.

The eye is blackest around the edges and it has a white highlight. Add a line around the eyelid.

Only the darkest parts are painted solid black. Most of the coat is painted in shades of grey, to show the glossy highlights. A highlight on the knee of the nearest foreleg makes it stand out from the one behind as well as making it look glossy.

**Brushstrokes going in the direction of the growth of the coat make it look sleek and well groomed.**

**The jump is not drawn in great detail, so that the eye is attracted to the horse, which is the more important part of the picture.**

**By showing no background you can ensure that the horse and rider are the focus of attention.**

# Assorted animals

Over the next few pages is an assortment of animals. Some are drawn in realistic styles as well as cartoon styles, so that you can compare the techniques.

## A giraffe

An adult giraffe is about five metres (15ft) high. Draw it on a piece of paper that is higher than it is wide. (This is called "portrait" format.) This will emphasize the animal's tall proportions.

**Sketch the animal's roughly triangular body shape, as shown.**

**The head shape is a small triangle.**

**The neck makes up about half of the height.**

**A swishing tail adds a little movement to the picture.**

**When all the paint has dried, add dark grey shadows around the hooves and knees, and on the head.**

**Paint the giraffe with watercolours. First, damp the paper slightly with clean water. Then paint on a base of yellowish fawn.**

**Apply the dark brown patches while the base colour is still damp. The edges of the patches will merge with the base colour, giving the impression of a soft coat.**

**For a cartoon, exaggerate the length and flexibility of the neck.**

**Heavy-lidded eyes give a dopey expression.**

**Colour a cartoon giraffe with bright felt tips.**

**Create a strong outline with a black pen.**

## A zebra

A zebra is similar in shape to a horse but with a slightly shorter body and a shorter mane. No two zebras' patterns are identical.

**Using pencil, sketch the body shapes, then the markings.**

**Colour in the stripes using black paint or coloured pencil.**

**Add soft grey to areas that are in shadow, such as the tummy and under the neck.**

**The tail swishes to keep flies away.**

# An elephant

An elephant has a tough, wrinkly skin which can be tricky to draw convincingly. The one shown here is an African elephant. It has bigger ears than an Indian elephant. Using pencil, sketch the body and head shapes first, then the legs and ears, then the trunk and tail.

**Sketch faintly, so that the pencil marks will not show through on your picture.**

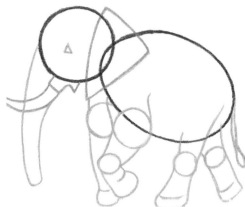

**Begin painting by applying a base wash of grey watercolour.**

**While the base wash is still damp, dab on some sand brown patches and dark grey shadows.**

**When the washes have dried, add wrinkles, using a fine brush.**

# A kangaroo

To emphasize the speed and forward momentum of a bounding kangaroo, draw it on a piece of paper that is wider than it is high. This is known as "landscape" format.

**The head is small compared to the rest of the body.**

**The body tapers towards the neck and is almost parallel to the ground.**

**Big, powerful hindquarters**

**Apply a thin wash of reddish brown watercolour. When this is dry, apply another coat of the same colour, but leave out the highlighted parts.**

**Add dark brown shadows to the body. Paint dark grey on features such as the eyes, ears and feet.**

**For a cartoon, exaggerate the size of the nose, paws and ears. Include the pouch, complete with a young kangaroo inside.**

# A hippopotamus

A hippopotamus is similar to an elephant in body shape, but it has a squatter body and stubbier legs. When on dry land, it holds its head down low. Begin painting by applying a wash of pinkish brown watercolour.

**Touches of white on the face and parts of the body make the skin look wet and shiny.**

**Add patches of grey to darker areas.**

# Animal cartoons

Cartoons can be used to highlight an animal's most obvious, memorable features. By showing the animal performing human actions and making human expressions, you can suggest its nature in the cartoon.

After sketching the animal's shape, go over the finished outline and the features with a black ink pen. Finally, colour it in, using felt tips.

## A toucan

The large, brightly coloured beak and staring eyes of a toucan make it a good subject for a cartoon. Fill in the body with black only, to emphasize its sleekness and to set off the brightness of the beak.

## A camel

For a cartoon camel, show the humped back, knobbly knees, large lips and shaggy fur around the neck.

**Half-closed eyes give the camel an arrogant expression.**

## An elephant

Real elephants do not stand on their hind legs but the posture of this cartoon elephant has been adapted to make it look as if it is dancing.

**Pink skin gives an unreal effect.**

**A smiling face makes the elephant look almost human.**

## A panda

A panda's vivid, contrasting markings can make a striking cartoon. You could draw one surrounded by bamboo shoots.

**A happy face shows that the panda is enjoying its food.**

## A rhinoceros

Real rhinoceroses are not blue, but you can make a cartoon version any colour you like. This will help to make the picture eye-catching.

## A hippopotamus

For a cartoon hippo, emphasize the size and shape of its jaw and make its legs short and fat. Compare this cartoon with the hippo on the previous page.

## An aardvark

**In real life, an aardvark is brownish, not blue.**

An aardvark's strange but fairly simple shape makes it a good subject for a cartoon. The most prominent features are the long snout and big ears.

# Hedgehogs

For a cartoon hedgehog, emphasize its rounded body, pointed snout and prickly covering. Begin by sketching oval shapes for the body and head, with a small circle for the nose.

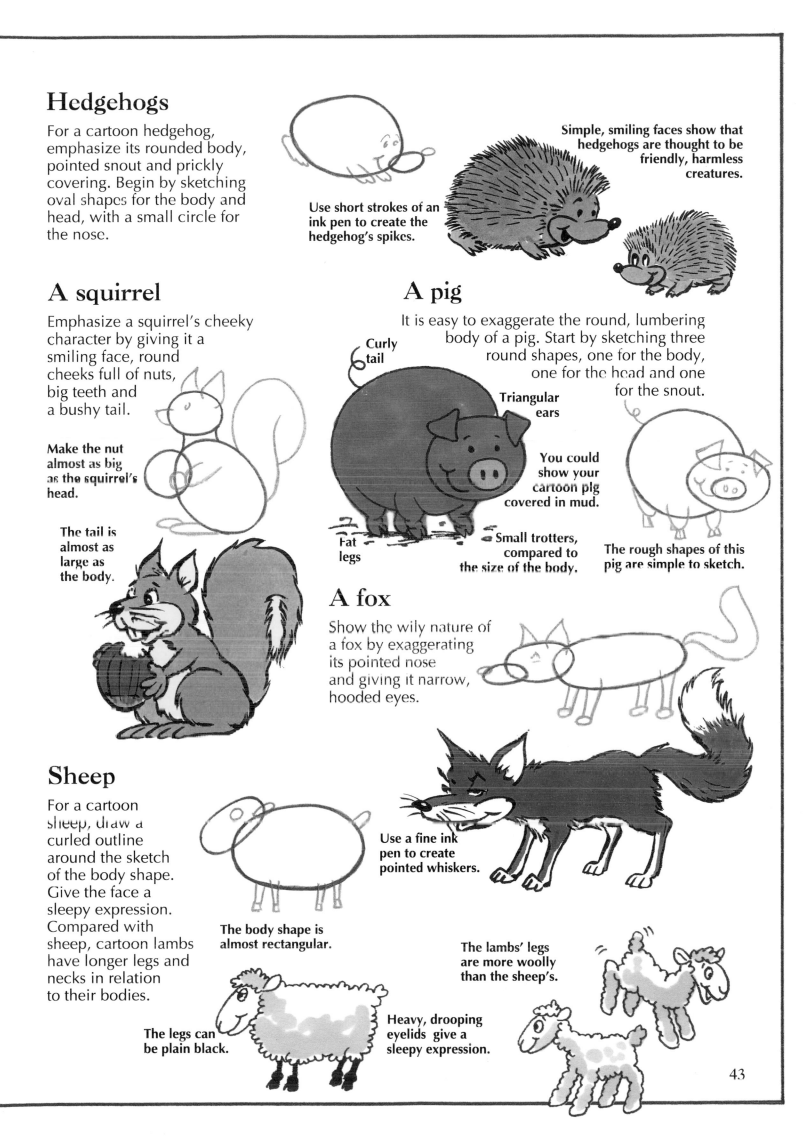

Use short strokes of an ink pen to create the hedgehog's spikes.

Simple, smiling faces show that hedgehogs are thought to be friendly, harmless creatures.

# A squirrel

Emphasize a squirrel's cheeky character by giving it a smiling face, round cheeks full of nuts, big teeth and a bushy tail.

Make the nut almost as big as the squirrel's head.

The tail is almost as large as the body.

# A pig

It is easy to exaggerate the round, lumbering body of a pig. Start by sketching three round shapes, one for the body, one for the head and one for the snout.

Curly tail

Triangular ears

You could show your cartoon pig covered in mud.

Fat legs

Small trotters, compared to the size of the body.

The rough shapes of this pig are simple to sketch.

# A fox

Show the wily nature of a fox by exaggerating its pointed nose and giving it narrow, hooded eyes.

Use a fine ink pen to create pointed whiskers.

# Sheep

For a cartoon sheep, draw a curled outline around the sketch of the body shape. Give the face a sleepy expression. Compared with sheep, cartoon lambs have longer legs and necks in relation to their bodies.

The body shape is almost rectangular.

The legs can be plain black.

Heavy, drooping eyelids give a sleepy expression.

The lambs' legs are more woolly than the sheep's.

# Sea creatures

Because most sea creatures are so different in shape to land animals, they can be challenging to draw, either in a realistic style or as cartoons.

## A turtle

A turtle's shape is made up of an oval for the body and leaf shapes for the flippers and head. The shell looks like armour plating.

**Paint the body with watercolours, starting with a wash of the lightest colour.**

**Leave white highlights on the shell to show where it catches the light.**

## A seahorse

Sketch a seahorse's body with curling shapes. The shape of the head resembles that of a horse. The tail curls around on itself.

**Shade the delicate fins using coloured pencils.**

**Highlight the ridges on the body with white paint.**

## A shark

For a cartoon shark, start with this sleek shape. Place a backward-facing fin in the middle of the back. Then position the other fins, the gills and the facial features.

**Cuts in the tail show that this shark has fought many battles.**

**A fierce, evil look in the eye shows that this shark is out to catch its dinner.**

**Sharp, triangular teeth slope backwards.**

## Tropical fish

The tropical fish on the left show variations on the fish shape and give some ideas for markings. Give them exotic fins and tails.

## A giant octopus

For a giant octopus, sketch an egg-shaped head and show as many of its eight tentacles as you can.

**The tentacles are covered in suckers.**

# Flying animals

Birds and other flying animals can be particularly difficult to draw in detail because you cannot get very close to them, and because they do not keep still. If you are drawing them from life, make quick sketches before you draw them in detail. Alternatively, copy them from photos in books, or take your own photographs to refer to as you draw.

## Birds

Most birds share certain characteristics, such as feathers and a streamlined shape. The wings are attached to the spine, so they come out of the top of the body, not the sides. You could try adapting the basic shapes of the terns below to draw other birds in flight.

**The wings always bend in the same place and curve slightly backwards.**

## Bats

Bats can be drawn as silhouettes, with simple faces added. Fill in the shapes with black felt tip.

**On the downstroke, the wings curve a lot.**

**For shadows, use touches of very pale bluish grey.**

## Chickens

To draw a hen, begin with the red shapes. Then draw the tail, beak and comb, shown in blue. Lastly, sketch the legs and feet. Use long curves for the shapes of a cockerel's body. It has a bigger comb than a hen and more dramatic colouring.

**Paint the cockerel's comb bright red.**

**To paint the hen with watercolours, begin with a pale brown wash. Then build darker patches on top.**

## Butterflies

To see how to draw butterflies in different positions, copy the red and green shapes on paper and cut them out. Fold it to the position you want, then look at it as you draw.

**These butterflies were decorated using pastels. These give a soft, powdery look. You can use coloured pencils instead.**

45

# Creepy crawlies

To show the fine details on creepy crawlies'
bodies, such as tiny hairs or delicate markings,
draw the animals large, as if you were close to
them or magnifying them.

**First, sketch the
body. Then add
the legs and
antennae.**

**This ant is
carrying
a leaf.**

## An ant

Like all insects, an ant has six legs and its body
is divided into three parts, called the head,
thorax and abdomen. This ant is brown but there
are other varieties of ant which are black or red.

Head

Thorax

Abdomen

**Make the ant look solid by
leaving white highlights
and adding dark shadows.**

## A garden spider

Spiders' oval body parts and
long, thin legs are simple to
sketch. The spider shown here
is a garden spider. Its back
has a white cross on it.

**Either leave the cross unpainted,
or, as here, paint the whole
spider brown and add the cross
last, in gouache.**

**Paint smudgy washes of
green and grey for the
background. With
a thin brush, paint the
web on top, using
gouache.**

**Sketch the body
sections first,
then add eight
spindly legs.**

**Build up darker
shades on top of a
light wash of watercolour.**

**Add hairs to
the legs, using
a fine brush.**

## A snail

A snail's shell is spiralled in an anticlockwise
direction. The spiral exists inside the shell,
forming a long chamber which supports the
snail's soft body.

**Sketch the
shell first.**

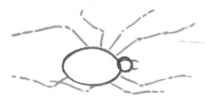

**Show the shell's
spirals in the
rough sketch.**

**Using thin, white watercolour,
paint a glistening trail
of slime behind
the snail.**

**Highlights show
that the shell is
hard, shiny
and finely
ridged.**

## A cockroach

A cockroach's shell is made up of segments. This
allows the cockroach greater flexibility than if the
shell was formed from a single piece.

**Cover the cockroach, except
for highlights, with a pale
brown wash. Build up
darker colours on the
sides and front.**

**Highlights
show that
the shell is
hard and
reflective.**

**Use black
watercolour
for the darkest
shadows.**

**Streaks of
thin, light brown
watercolour, with darker
pencil streaks on top,
suggest a wooden surface.**

# GHOSTS AND MONSTERS

Because there are so many different accounts of what ghosts and monsters look like, you can draw them in just about any style or shape that you can imagine. There are lots of examples from the worlds of myth and legend that can inspire your pictures, such as stories of vampires, walking skeletons and dragons. You could even become a new Frankenstein and create your own monster.

In this section you will come across some imaginative ways to create outlines or put colour on a picture. The subjects are well suited to these techniques, since the pictures are less realistic than, say, drawings of animals and people, and dramatic special effects can work well.

# Ghosts

A conventional way to draw ghosts is to show them as floating shapes. These can look very effective shown as simple outlines and filled in with soft, blended watercolours.

**Ghostly shapes like these can be shown in any position, even flying upside-down.**

**Draw the shape lightly, in pencil. Make it big so that you have a large surface to paint on.**

**Brush the shape with clean water. Then add streaks of paint on top.**

**The wet paints will blend and make different colours where they mix.**

**For a really spooky effect leave rough, unpainted spaces for the eyes and mouth.**

**A blurred trail of light yellow coming from the mouth looks like ghostly ectoplasm.**

**Rough, haphazard edges make the ghost look less distinct, but also more sinister.**

## Fiery ghost

You can use ghostly shapes cut out from pieces of thin cardboard to create dramatic pictures, like the fiery ghost shown above.

**Put the cut-out shape on a smooth surface. Place a clean sheet of paper over the cut-out.**

**Rub all over the paper with two or three different wax crayons. Take care not to move the cut-out.**

**Go over the top part again with a dark crayon, so the ghost appears to fade away at the bottom.**

## Sheet ghosts

The idea that ghosts are like figures draped in flowing sheets probably came about because the dead used to be buried in white robes, called shrouds. Follow these tips to create a sheet ghost that looks as if it is floating along.

**Draw a stick-person in pencil. Add a sheet around the shape with a felt tip. Erase the pencil lines.**

**Draw thin black lines to show the folds of the sheet. Add a hint of shading with a coloured pencil.**

**Make the bottom of the sheet into a point to make the ghost look as if it is floating. Add dark eyes and a mouth.**

## Ghostly shadows

You can create funny effects by giving a shadow its own identity, separate from the person that it belongs to.

**Use solid blocks of dark shading to fill in the shadows.**

You could think up pictures of your own, showing mischievous shadows playing sneaky tricks on their owners.

**The expression on the face shows that the person senses a ghostly presence.**

## Japanese ghost

The Ancient Japanese used to believe that people who had led evil lives came back as ghosts. As a punishment for their wickedness, their legs were always in flames.

**First, sketch the ghost's bent-over body, using curling, rounded shapes.**

**Add the shape of the sleeves, shown here in blue.**

**Finally, sketch the facial expression and the shape of the flames.**

**Use black felt tip to go over the outline.**

**A loosely applied patch of yellow felt tip shows the heat of the fire.**

**Paint thin curls of red gouache over the yellow patch, to show the shapes of the flames.**

## See-through ghosts

To draw see-through ghosts, begin by sketching background shapes, such as the room, chair and door shown here, in pencil. Then go over the background shapes using waterproof ink, such as a ball point pen. Next draw the ghosts' outlines, using wax crayon.

Paint a thin layer of water over the whole picture. While the paper is still wet, paint streaks of watercolour on it.

# Skeletons and spooks

Skeletons always look sinister, with their hollow eyes and bared teeth, but the ones here also look amusing, because they are so ungainly.

These skeletons have been simplified, to make them easy to draw and more fun to look at. You could simplify skeletons in your own way, to suit your drawing style.

**Sketch the shape of the skeleton's pose. Draw the major bones only, to keep the picture simple.**

**Use very pale shading to give the skeleton some shape and texture.**

**You might like to imagine a setting for this skeleton, such as a dark, damp dungeon.**

**A real human skeleton contains over 200 bones.**

**For a skull, first draw the dome of the head and the eye sockets.**

**Next, add the jaw and the teeth. Show the teeth in a fixed grin.**

**Colour the eye sockets black and add a black triangle for the nose.**

**The spine is made up of lots of small bones. Draw them close together, but not touching.**

**Ribs curve and get shorter near the waist.**

You could show your skeletons in a selection of poses, such as those in the sketches above and in the picture on the right.

**This bone, called the pelvis, connects the legs to the spine.**

**Use pale blue and creamy yellow to colour the skeleton.**

**For a supernatural effect, draw the bones slightly apart, floating independently.**

**Feet and hands contain lots of small bones.**

## Grinning skull

To draw this skull, first copy the outline of the picture and go around it with a black pen. Colour it using bright colours, with murkier shadows. Add details using fine red and black lines.

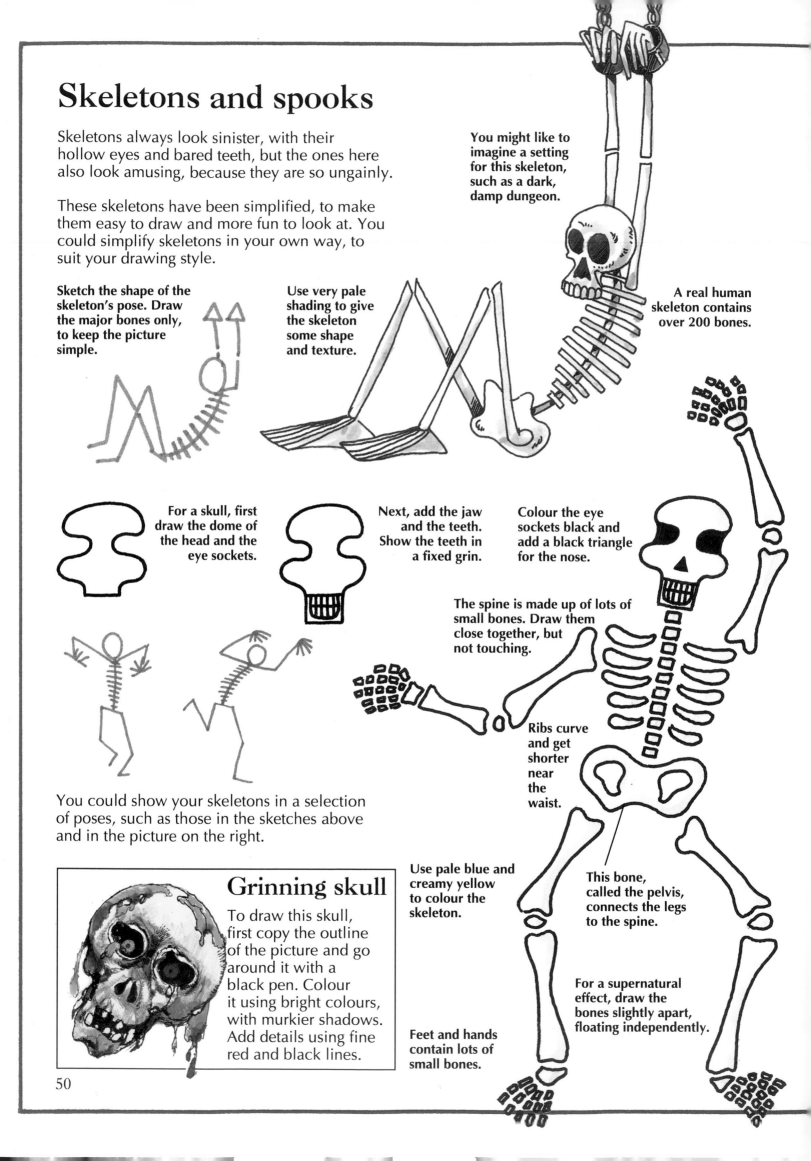

# Chinese ghost

In Ancient China, murdered people were said to return as ghosts, appearing from a shapeless cloud and surrounded by green light. To draw this picture, first copy the outlines below. Then sketch the details of its facial features and clothes.

Colour the ghost using a blend of blue, green and yellow coloured pencils.

The ghost was said to have no chin.

Use black to shade the important features, such as the face and hair.

Draw the outline with slightly shaky lines.

Go over the finished outlines with green and grey lines.

Ignore the ghost's outline when you show the green light. Instead, concentrate on making the light appear to billow and swirl. This will make the ghost's shape appear indistinct and sinister.

Curled blue lines emphasize the cloud shapes.

Gently fade the clouds at the edge of the drawing, to complete the billowing, gas-like effect.

# Barquest

This phantom dog, called Barquest, is said to be found near graveyards in France. Seeing it is supposed to mean certain death. Draw the outline of the ghost's shape, shown below, in pencil.

Sketch Barquest crouching down, about to terrify a victim.

Give Barquest demonic, staring eyes.

Create tufts of fur by doing close strokes with a black ink pen.

A combination of thick fur and bald patches makes Barquest look mangy.

Shade the thickest areas of fur with black ink. Use an ink pen to show individual tufts.

Where the outline is visible through the fur, go over it in ink. Then erase the pencil outline.

51

# Monster shapes

When inventing monsters, a useful starting point can be to base them on the shapes of real creatures. These pages show a few of the creatures that you can draw by following this idea. For example, the creature below is based on a dinosaur, while the one further down the page looks a little like a cat.

**Red eyes indicate that the monster is dangerous.**

**Sharp teeth, spines and a forked tongue make the monster look like a dragon.**

**Jagged markings reinforce the vicious look of the creature.**

**Some dangerous snakes have markings like these.**

**The tail has a weapon-like point.**

**To make the patterns look strong and memorable decorate the monster using bright felt tips.**

A monster that is drawn with straight lines only is likely to look fierce. Jagged spikes on its back add to the dangerous look. If you mix angular shapes with a friendly face (as below) you can create a monster that might be friendly, but could also turn vicious.

**Wriggly shapes can look unpleasant.**

**For a truly nightmarish monster, combine the long, slithery shape of a snake with a large, fierce head.**

**This monster has five legs. Your creatures can have unrealistic numbers of legs.**

**Frowning eyebrows and mean, narrow eyes look angry.**

**Deadly-looking fangs**

## Furry monster

Creatures with fuzzy shapes are more likely to look funny than frightening. This monster is based on a ball of fluff rather than an animal.

**Draw the shape of the nose and eyes first.**

**Use a soft pencil to draw the fur.**

**Smudge the fur with your finger to make it look soft.**

**Paint the eyes with white gouache. When dry, add the pupils in pencil.**

**Use red felt tip for the boots and nose.**

# Frightening fish

Invent a frightening fish monster by drawing the shape of a big fish, with a huge mouth and sharp teeth.

For the skin, first paint your fish with water or very watery colour. While it is still wet, dab on blobs of bright paint. The blobs will blend to give mottled markings.

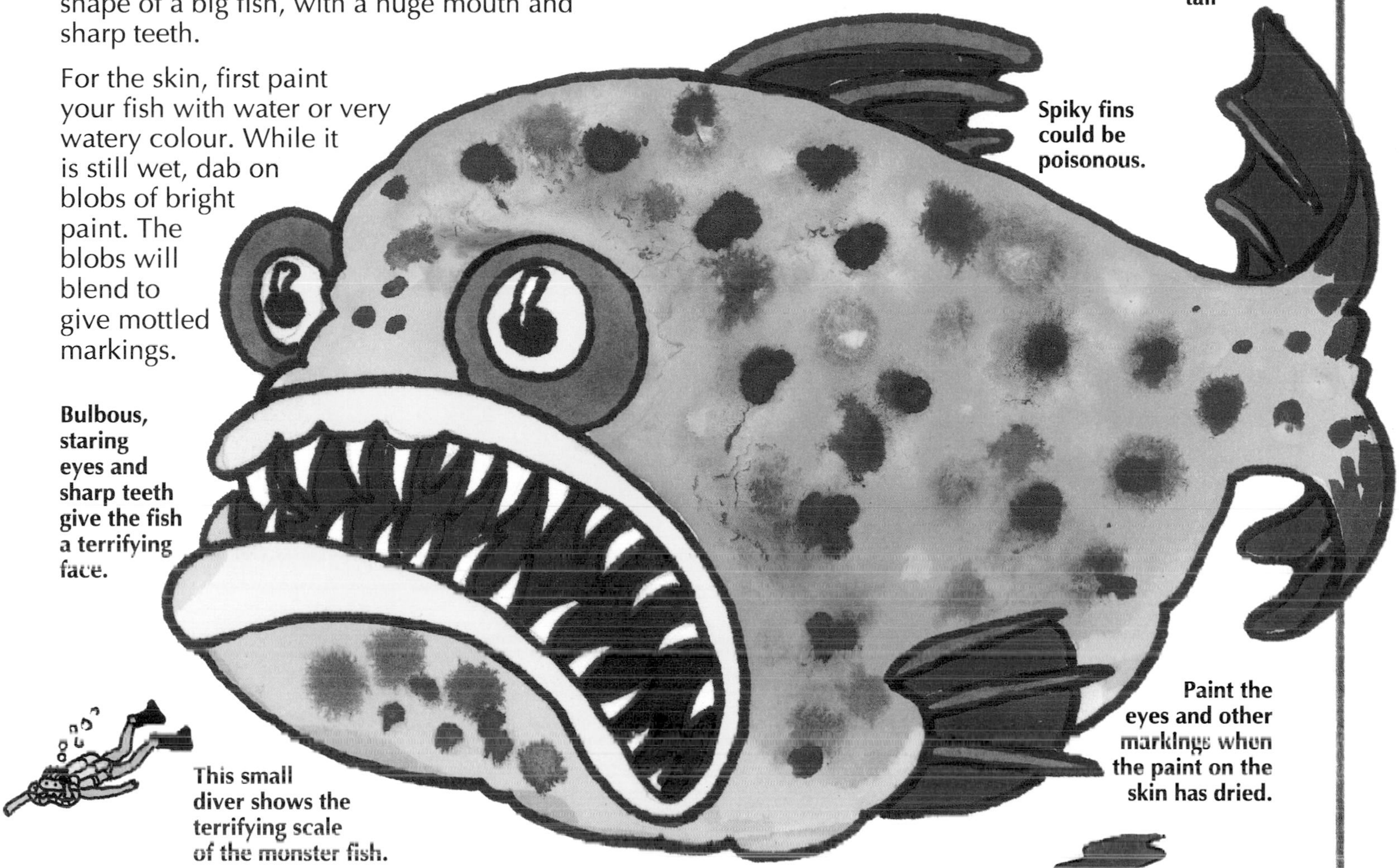

**Bulbous, staring eyes and sharp teeth give the fish a terrifying face.**

**Powerful tail**

**Spiky fins could be poisonous.**

**Paint the eyes and other markings when the paint on the skin has dried.**

**This small diver shows the terrifying scale of the monster fish.**

# Giant octopus

This giant octopus is splashing in a cloud of its own dark ink so you cannot see how big it is or where all of its eight tentacles are.

When you have sketched the octopus in pencil, paint a layer of light shading on the undersides of the tentacles. Then paint the eye red. When the paint has dried, add the black areas.

**A red eye makes the octopus look eerie and dangerous.**

**White stripes, added last, make the octopus look striking and help to show the curved shape of the tentacles.**

**Tentacles twist and curl.**

**There are suckers on the underside of each tentacle.**

53

# Dragons and ghouls

Dragons are imaginary monsters that originated in Far Eastern countries such as China. They can look very dangerous because they breathe fire, have sharp fangs, powerful jaws, and strong limbs and a tail for clouting their prey. They can fly, so they can attack from above. However, they can be simple to draw, as this example shows.

Sketch the body and head shapes. Then draw the neck, tail and leg shapes.

Add two fan-shaped wings, one on either side of the body.

Spines down the back of the neck.

Give the dragon a large mouth with sharp teeth, bulging eyes and big nostrils.

Add claws to the legs.

A coiled tail suggests that this dragon is about to lash out at something.

Apply a base wash of light green watercolour to all parts except the eyes, mouth, teeth and claws. When this is dry, add dark green markings on the body.

Leave the wings light green but add darker green for the bones.

You could paint your dragon with any colours and patterns you want.

Paint the fiery breath yellow. Before this is completely dry, add red inside and around the dragon's mouth.

Paint darker green shadows on the lower parts of the body and just in front of the legs.

In this picture, the markings were added by dipping a finger in thick green paint and dabbing fingerprints over the body, to look like scales.

## Vac-dragon

The monster on the right is a vac-dragon, a cross between a dragon and a vacuum cleaner. You could invent other creatures that are a mixture of traditional monsters and mechanical objects.

Evil eyes

Vacuum pipe becomes a flexible neck.

The sucking part becomes a head with a greedy, gaping mouth.

Cord and plug make a tail.

Clawed feet help to make the vacuum cleaner look more like a dragon.

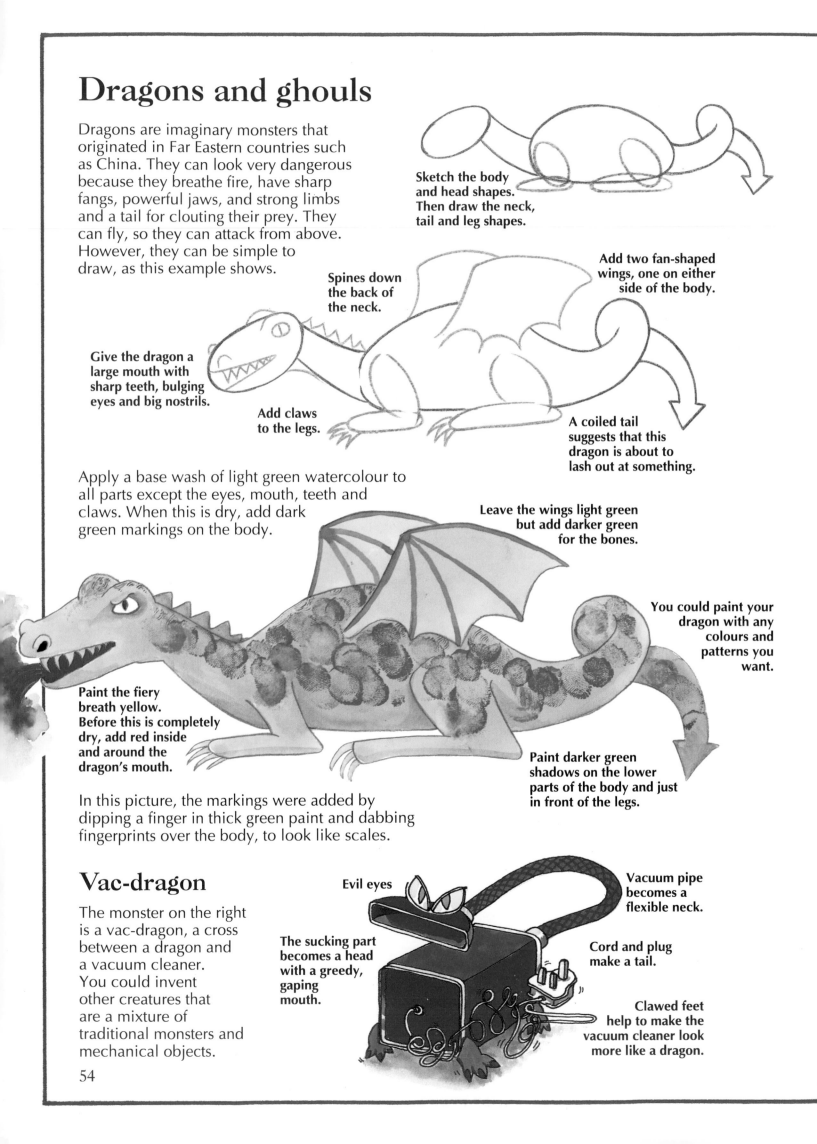

54

# Gruesome ghoul

Ghouls are evil spirits who first featured in Middle Eastern folklore. Their name comes from the Arab word *gul,* meaning "desert demon". To draw this ghoul, first copy the outlines shown on the right, using pencil.

**First, draw the shape of the tail and the back. Then sketch the bent legs, head and the arms.**

**Add the bony structure of the wings, plus the ears and the mouth.**

**Include details like the outline of the wings.**

**This creature was painted with coloured inks.**

**Before painting, go around the outline with a fine ink pen and add details such as the scales and shading on the wings. Erase any pencil lines.**

**For a weird effect allow colours to bleed across more than one part of the body. For example, red runs across the head and the upper body, while the green on the left wing also runs across the left arm.**

## Cartoon dragon

To create a harmless-looking cartoon dragon, you could use the style shown on the right. Use bright watercolours, with only a little water, so that the effect is strong. Allow the damp colours to merge with one another to create soft edges.

**Kind-looking eyes and a dopey smile.**

**Arms are outstretched in an open, friendly gesture.**

**Loud, clashing colours make the creature look clown-like.**

# Human monsters

Many monsters are either all or part human. Some, such as Frankenstein's monster and Count Dracula, are characters from books. Others are characters from ancient legends.

## Werewolves

Werewolves are human beings who change into savage, wolf-like creatures when there is a full moon. They live on human flesh and can only be killed by a silver bullet or knife. If they are buried they become vampires.

**Using a pencil, sketch the shapes of the werewolf's head, followed by its shoulders and clothes. Then sketch the rough shapes of its facial features, hair and ears.**

**Add details as shown in green. Then use a black pen to draw the hair and outline the features. Draw wrinkled skin using short lines.**

**Complete the picture with loose patches of shade, using coloured pencils.**

## Frankenstein's monster

In the book *Frankenstein*, Baron Frankenstein puts together a man from various parts of other people, and brings him to life artificially. The monster grows to hate the Baron and eventually kills him.

**The head is lit from above, to emphasize the hollows in the face.**

**Fill in the blocks of shade with black felt tip.**

**Stitches show where the creature was joined together.**

## Witches

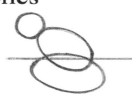

Witches are supposed to be able to cast spells and cause mischief. To draw a silhouette of a witch, begin by sketching her head, body and broomstick.

Add details until you have a complete outline of the flying witch. Go over the outline with black felt tip. Then fill in the shape.

Draw a circle around the witch, to show her flying past a full moon. Black felt tip outside the circle shows the night sky.

# Dracula

Vampires have existed for centuries in the folklore of various countries. The most famous vampire of all is Count Dracula. He first appeared in a book by Bram Stoker in 1897.

To sketch Dracula, first draw the shapes shown in red. Then add the shapes shown in green.

Add red details to the mouth and eyes.

Shade the skin and waistcoat with coloured pencils.

Use thick black gouache or poster paint on parts such as the outside of the hair, and the cloak.

Use a fine ink pen to add detail to the clothes and skin and to draw the pattern around the top of the waistcoat.

Use red poster paint on the inside of the cloak and the top of the waistcoat.

## Dracula's story

In Bram Stoker's story *Dracula*, Count Dracula lives in a huge, rambling castle in Transylvania, a region in Romania in eastern Europe. He kills people by biting their necks and then drinking their blood. His dead victims become vampires as well. Dracula hatches a plan to fill the world with vampires and decides to start in England. He travels there by ship, killing all the crew and drinking their blood. He terrorizes London with a wave of vampire attacks but is chased back to Transylvania. Eventually, he is killed in Transylvania by being stabbed with a silver knife through the heart.

Paint the trousers grey. Let this dry, then add black stripes.

# Vampire cartoons

Vampires make good cartoons because they have strong identifying features, such as their fangs and cloaks, which can be exaggerated and caricatured. Also, the areas of contrasting black and red on a vampire help to make striking pictures.

**Greenish skin gives Dracula a sickly look.**

**A piercing stare makes Dracula look demonic.**

To draw a cartoon of Count Dracula, start by sketching the rough shapes shown on the right. Sketch a stick figure for his body, then draw a cloak around the body. Complete the picture with felt tips.

**Parts of the cloak that catch the light are dark blue.**

You can draw cartoons of vampires in characteristic poses, such as those shown on the right. Other ideas might be to show him relaxing in his coffin or watching horror movies on television.

**Dracula skulking furtively.**

**Dracula gleefully about to pounce.**

**Dracula swooping down on his prey.**

## Dracula's expressions

Dracula is usually shown as a person who does not laugh, cry or show any emotions at all. However, in cartoons, you can show him in more expressive moods. Here are a few examples, but you could invent expressions to show plenty of other moods such as sadness or confusion.

**Sly**

**Thirsty**

**Gleeful**

**Angry**

**Tired**

**Thoughtful**

**Shifty**

Here are some body shapes that you could use or adapt in your pictures, to show Dracula's poses. You could combine these with the heads shown above to make complete pictures.

**Tiptoeing**

**Dancing**

**Jumping**

**Lurking**

58

# More cartoon creeps

The cartoon creeps shown here are examples of ways to portray everyday people and things as if they are sinister, but funny. Complete the cartoons with felt tip pens.

**Vampire bats**

**Spooky owl**

**Blood-curdling butler**

**Batty clock**

**Transylvanian castle**

**Talking heads**

**Grisly graveyard**

**Bone chair**

**Bat walking stick.** Perhaps Dracula uses this when he goes out for a stroll.

This pair of vampire rats could lurk in Dracula's cellar in Transylvania.

**Bone china**

You could show these vampire characters in a scene together with Dracula. Alternatively, invent a comic strip for them to star in. (For tips on drawing comic strips, see pages 21 and 114.)

**Granny Vampire and her vampire cat**

**Fang the spider**

# A unicorn

Monsters from myths and legend can be drawn so that they have a fantastic, dream-like quality. To draw this unicorn, start as if it were an ordinary horse. The rearing pose on page 36 might help you to sketch the pose correctly. The unicorn has been drawn from a low angle, to make it look imposing. This adds to the larger-than-life feeling of the picture.

**A very dark eye with a white highlight looks luminous and intelligent.**

**There is a small beard on the chin.**

**The raised head and ears held back make the unicorn look proud and defiant.**

**Curved, swirling lines for the thick mane and forelock give a romantic, magical look to the head.**

**The tail is like a lion's: long, smooth and muscular, with just a tassel of curly hair at the end.**

**The hooves are split, or cloven, like a goat's. There is wavy, silky hair on the fetlocks.**

**Soft blue shading with watercolour makes the coat look clean and adds a shimmering, mysterious effect.**

**Follow the diagram below when you do your sketch. Do the red shapes first, then the green shapes, then the blue.**

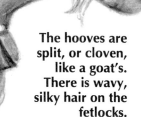

**Touches of light fawn watercolour make the figure look as if it is glowing magically.**

A unicorn is a mythical creature that first appeared in drawings by people in the Middle East. Since then it has appeared in the literature of Ancient Greece and the art of the Middle Ages. It was said to be a rare, beautiful but wild animal that could only be tamed by a young girl.

**To create deep shadows between the back legs and on the belly, apply the darkest shades last.**

60

# ROBOTS, ALIENS AND SPACECRAFT

Drawing robots and aliens presents a mixture of challenges. A robot has a hard, shiny surface like a machine, but its body parts might resemble those of a human being. An alien can be any shape at all, but its body covering might be scaly, or slimy like a reptile. The skills you build up in drawing people, machines and animals can all come in useful when drawing robots and aliens.

Also in this section you can find out how to create transport for robots and aliens, as well as real spacecraft. Instructions show you how to draw the Space Shuttle, Saturn 5 (the American rocket which took the first men to the Moon) and a Russian Soyuz rocket. These machines have immense power and as well as drawing the spacecraft themselves, you can have fun colouring the flames and smoke that billow from their exhaust systems.

# First robots

You can gain inspiration for the designs of all kinds of robots by looking at ordinary objects. As an example, the robot on this page is based on a tin can.

Start with a pencil sketch of a tin can shape. Use a ruler to make the sides straight. The ovals at the top and bottom give the can its round shape.

Add a dome for the head. You could use a pair of compasses for this. Add an eye window, antennae, a seam line and some tiny bolts, all shown below in red.

When you have sketched the shapes, erase the lines shown by green dashes.

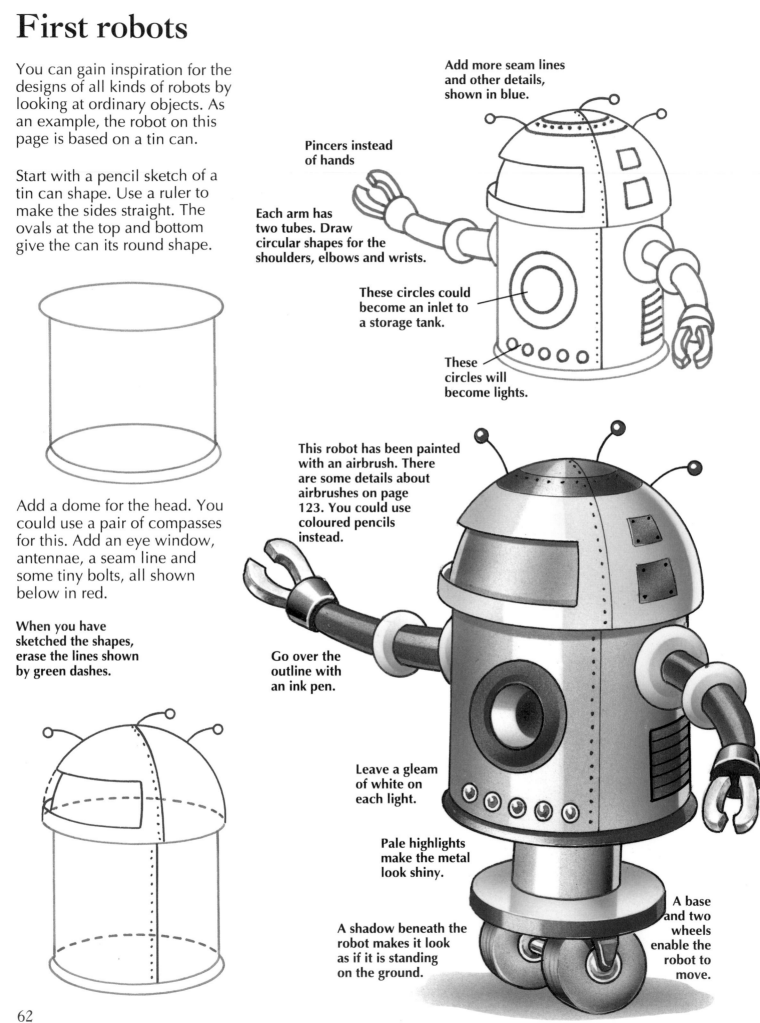

Add more seam lines and other details, shown in blue.

Pincers instead of hands

Each arm has two tubes. Draw circular shapes for the shoulders, elbows and wrists.

These circles could become an inlet to a storage tank.

These circles will become lights.

This robot has been painted with an airbrush. There are some details about airbrushes on page 123. You could use coloured pencils instead.

Go over the outline with an ink pen.

Leave a gleam of white on each light.

Pale highlights make the metal look shiny.

A shadow beneath the robot makes it look as if it is standing on the ground.

A base and two wheels enable the robot to move.

# Household helpers

These two robots are well suited to their functions as household helpers. You could invent other robots to help with jobs around the house, such as cleaning dishes or ironing clothes. Give them body shapes and details that are appropriate to the tasks that they will perform.

These two robots were finished with coloured pencils. When colouring them in, build up the darker shades with lots of strokes, all in the same direction. Erase the parts that you want to look shiny.

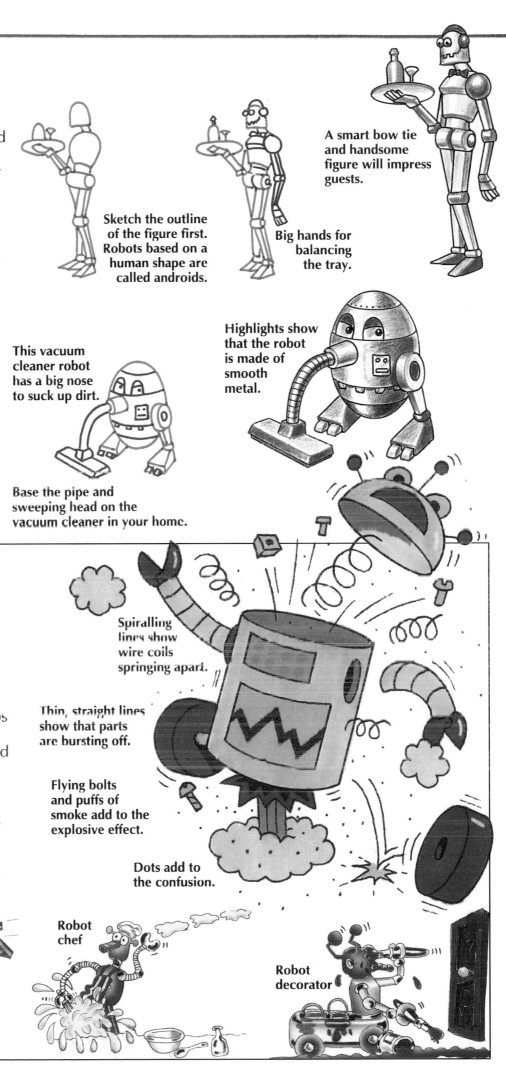

**Sketch the outline of the figure first. Robots based on a human shape are called androids.**

**A smart bow tie and handsome figure will impress guests.**

**Big hands for balancing the tray.**

**Highlights show that the robot is made of smooth metal.**

**This vacuum cleaner robot has a big nose to suck up dirt.**

**Large, egg-shaped body to store dirt.**

**Base the pipe and sweeping head on the vacuum cleaner in your home.**

# Robot malfunctions

These robots have all lost control of themselves due to malfunctions in their systems. You could create your own robots in crisis, either blowing up or falling apart. Alternatively, you could show them making a mess of the jobs they have been built for, like the examples below. You could show one making a disastrous attempt to tidy your room.

Cartoon-style pictures, such as these, are usually coloured in a bright, clean style. Use felt tips to create results like these.

**Spiralling lines show wire coils springing apart.**

**Thin, straight lines show that parts are bursting off.**

**Flying bolts and puffs of smoke add to the explosive effect.**

**Dots add to the confusion.**

**Lawnmower robot**

**Robot chef**

**Robot decorator**

# Androids

To draw and paint the imposing android on the opposite page, follow the instructions below. Before you paint the android, choose a strong colour for it and create a range of shades by mixing this colour with different amounts of white paint, as shown on the right. You will end up with four different shades, plus pure white.

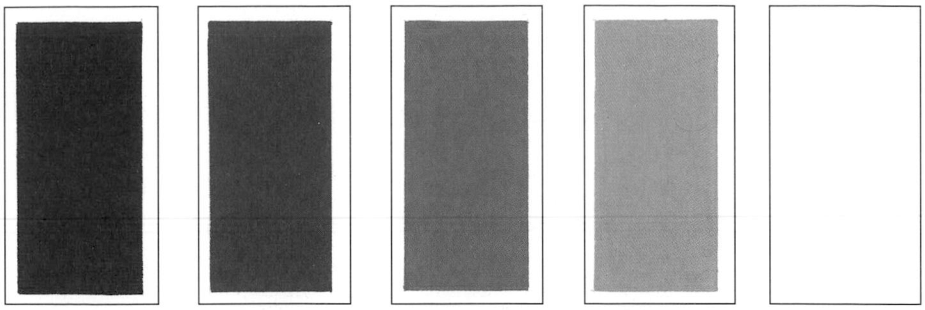

| Pure blue | 3/4 blue 1/4 white | 1/2 blue 1/2 white | 1/4 blue 3/4 white | Pure white |
|-----------|---------------------|---------------------|---------------------|------------|

**1**

Using pencil, start with a sketch of the outline. Press gently, so that you can erase the outline later.

To make the stance look powerful and threatening, position the feet wide apart.

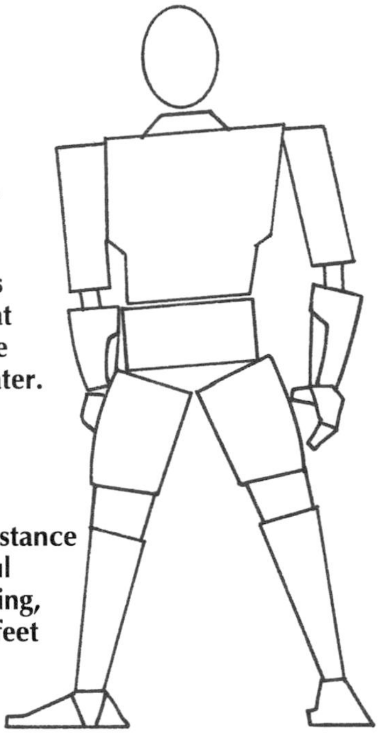

**2**

Give the android wide shoulders.

Tensed hands make it look as if it is about to grab its laser gun.

Give the android joints that would work, if it was constructed.

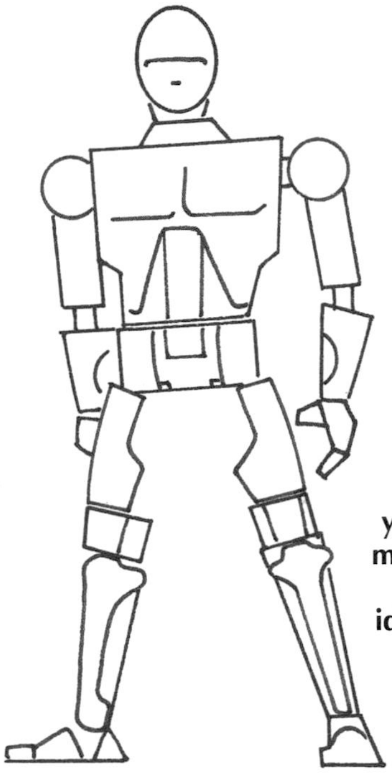

Start to add some detail and shape to parts of the body.

Androids that you have seen in movies or comics may give you ideas for features to add to your drawing.

**3**

The android's facial features are regular and geometric.

Details such as joints, lights, buttons and tubing, help to make the robot look more machine-like and convincing.

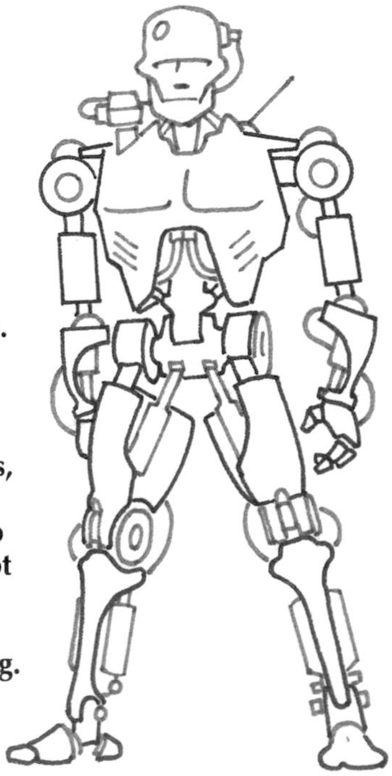

**4**

Before you start painting, decide which direction the light is coming from in your picture. This will help you decide which areas should be in shade and which should be highlighted. Here, the light is coming from the right.

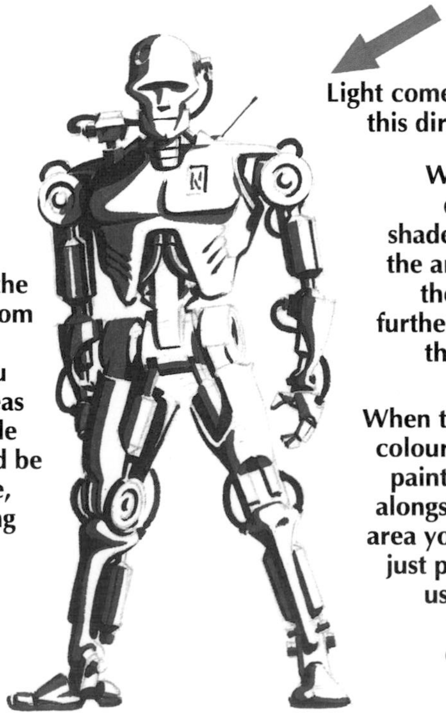

Light comes from this direction.

With the darkest shade, paint the areas on the robot furthest from the light.

When the first colour is dry, paint a strip alongside the area you have just painted, using the second darkest shade.

64

# Blending shades

Blending shades will make your picture look more realistic by making the curves of the body look smooth. To blend shades, carefully apply tiny dots of the second shade along the edge of the first. Applying paint in dots is called stippling.

## 5

Next to the second shade, paint a band of the third shade. This band should be very thin. Blend the shades as described In the *Blending shades* section, above.

Let the paint dry. Then take the fourth shade and paint all remaining areas. Again, blend the sections of paint together.

Third shade

## 6

Add small amounts of pure white to the middle of the light areas. Don't overdo it, or you will lose the shiny effect.

For the brightest flashes of highlights, apply small, dense white blobs of paint.

For areas of less brilliant highlights, allow the blue paint to show through the white.

Slot for miniature disks, for programming the android for different tasks.

On the chest is a badge showing the manufacturer's logo. You could base a badge on your initials.

A camera, for filming events. The antenna on the other shoulder is used for transmitting the pictures.

Hydraulic pistons. Pressure in these rises and falls, causing the android's body parts to move.

Sturdy body plates protect the most important circuits and microprocessors.

Pipes pump oil into the pistons, causing them to move.

Some mechanisms, such as those on the arms and legs, are left exposed to allow easy access for servicing.

Large feet for stability.

# Alien characters

As no one has ever proved what an alien from another planet might look like, you can draw them with whatever features you want. You can make aliens cuddly, ferocious or sneaky. You could try to mix characteristics in your alien. The one here, for instance, looks daft and unthreatening, but it could also do some damage with its claws.

**Enormous ears make the alien look silly.**

**To create tones on the body parts, use two shades of each colour, one light and one dark.**

**Draw two large ovals, overlapping each other. Add circles for the hips and shoulders, then draw sticks for the limbs.**

**The legs get wider, like flared jeans.**

**First, go over all coloured areas with light coloured pencil. Go over shadows with a darker shade. Press harder to create darker shadows.**

**Next, add the bulging eyes, enormous mouth and two very long ears. Draw shoulders, elbows and a belt, then add the alien's fingers and claws.**

**Go around the whole figure with a thin, dark outline, to make the figure stand out.**

**Although the claws look dangerous, the alien's silly smile and friendly posture prevent it from looking fierce.**

**Draw the lines shown in blue to add some extra details to the alien's clothes and body. Finally, colour it in, following the tips on the right.**

**The shiny appearance of the clothes makes them look hard, like an insect's shell.**

**For highlights, leave some areas white.**

# Alien faces

The alien on the page opposite is probably friendly, but what about the three aliens on this page? One of them looks definitely evil, but the other two are more difficult to assess. Their calm appearances could mean that they are your friends but they might be hiding the fact that they are about to destroy the Universe. By giving your aliens names as well as facial expressions, you will help them come to life.

## Colouring aliens

Because different colouring methods give a different quality of finish, you can use them to create various effects. Here are some examples of how a colouring method can subtly affect the final appearance of your aliens.

**Watercolours make Vultawk's skin seem smooth. This helps to give him a cold, slippery look.**

**Coloured pencils give Solero a soft-edged, gentle look. Curves at her neck look like warts.**

**Gouache makes Lord Hydlebar look bold. Leave a dark gap between his lips to show that he has no teeth.**

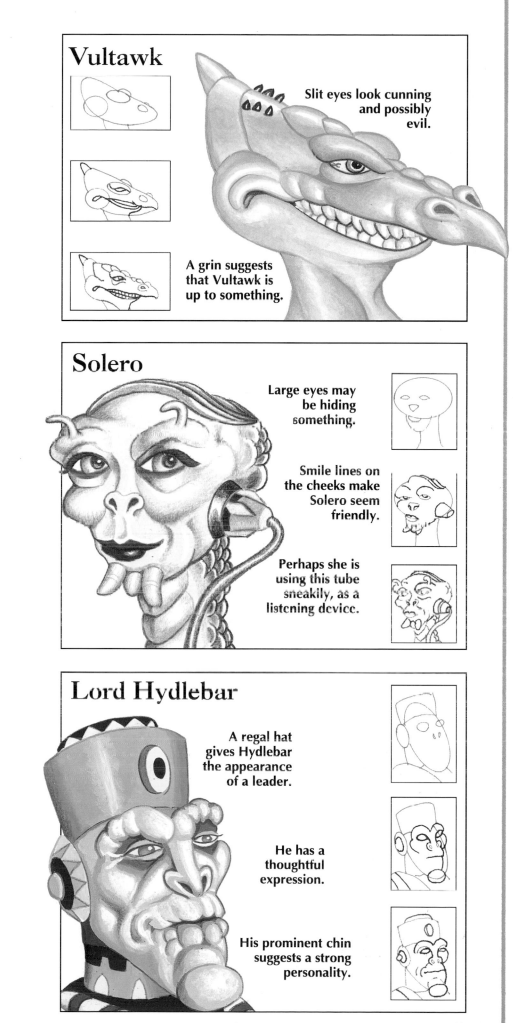

## Vultawk

**Slit eyes look cunning and possibly evil.**

**A grin suggests that Vultawk is up to something.**

## Solero

**Large eyes may be hiding something.**

**Smile lines on the cheeks make Solero seem friendly.**

**Perhaps she is using this tube sneakily, as a listening device.**

## Lord Hydlebar

**A regal hat gives Hydlebar the appearance of a leader.**

**He has a thoughtful expression.**

**His prominent chin suggests a strong personality.**

# Aliens in action

You can make your pictures of aliens look animated by showing the creatures on the move. For example, this picture catches the alien in the middle of a dance movement. His arms swinging one way while he is looking the other way give the picture energy. One foot raised high off the floor also gives a sense of movement.

The alien's body looks well-balanced, because although the arms and leg are swinging wildly, the head and trunk are positioned directly over the foot on the floor.

**The head, right knee and right foot are in a straight line.**

**A sharp angle at the left knee makes the raised leg look dramatic.**

**These spines are similar to those found on some reptiles.**

**The bug-eyed smile shows that the alien is happy and makes it look funny.**

**Knobbly knees add a comical touch to any picture.**

**The pincers are like a crab's claws.**

**Bright colours help to bring life to the picture.**

**The rounded effect on the limbs and body is achieved by using the lightest colour on the area nearest to you, and darker colours where the body curves away.**

This alien was coloured with an airbrush, although felt tips would give just as bright a picture. The finish will probably be flatter, though.

Colours that contrast can stop a picture from looking messy. However, they should not all compete in brightness. Here, the spotted orange costume is the brightest, so it stands out and contrasts with the green limbs.

## Alien eyes

You can change your alien's mood by adding just a couple of lines to its eyes.

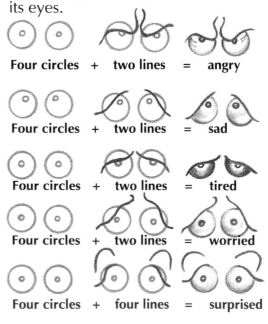

Four circles + two lines = angry

Four circles + two lines = sad

Four circles + two lines = tired

Four circles + two lines = worried

Four circles + four lines = surprised

68

# Creepy alien

To make a creepy alien, you can borrow features from the scariest real creatures you have seen, such as creepy crawlies, sea animals and reptiles. The alien shown here is based on a spider.

To paint it, apply a layer of pale watercolour. Let it dry, then add shading in coloured pencil, in a deeper shade. Draw dark hairs on top. Bald patches and tufts of hair look creepier than hair all over the body.

**Extra features such as a third eye, make the creature look unique.**

**Draw a patchy growth of ragged, individual hairs.**

**Each leg is made up of three tubes.**

**Make the joints out of circles.**

**Add creepy features, such as folds of baggy skin.**

**Make pointed feet, as shown in red.**

# Leapfrogger

This creepy alien moves in a leapfrogging motion. Perhaps it is chasing its next meal. Paint the skin with watercolours. Let the paint dry, then add dabs of white paint to look as if light is glistening on the alien's wet skin.

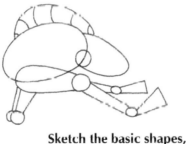

**Sketch the basic shapes, starting with the main body shapes. Next, add limbs and joints.**

**Complete your sketch by adding the details shown in red, in pencil.**

**Webbed hands and feet show that the alien is a good swimmer, as well as being able to move around on land.**

**Add a dot of white to its eye, to make it glisten.**

**A dark outline makes the alien stand out.**

**Dark parts are in shadow.**

# Alien friends

You can turn your friends into aliens. Start by drawing a caricature (see page 20).

**In this caricature, the person's red hair, ears and long chin have been exaggerated.**

Now draw an alien with these features, exaggerated even further and coloured in an extraordinary, alien way.

**This subject has been given antennae and outlandish blue and orange colouring.**

Here are some more caricatures with their alien versions next to them.

# Alien spaceships

The design of an alien spaceship should depend on what you imagine it will be used for. For example, a police spaceship such as the one below needs to look fast and sturdy in order to provide the high performance necessary for chasing criminal aliens.

The spaceships on these pages were airbrushed, which gives them a very smooth finish suitable for shiny, high-tech materials. (For more information on airbrushing, see page 123.) As an alternative use gouache or poster paints for a strong, vivid look.

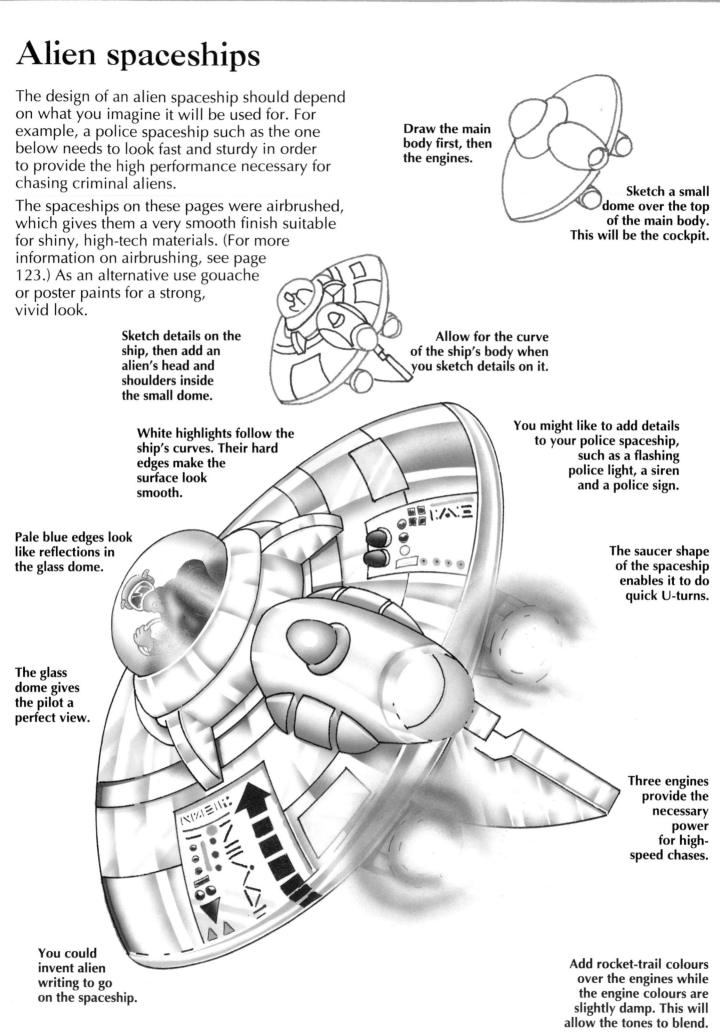

**Draw the main body first, then the engines.**

**Sketch a small dome over the top of the main body. This will be the cockpit.**

**Sketch details on the ship, then add an alien's head and shoulders inside the small dome.**

**Allow for the curve of the ship's body when you sketch details on it.**

**White highlights follow the ship's curves. Their hard edges make the surface look smooth.**

**You might like to add details to your police spaceship, such as a flashing police light, a siren and a police sign.**

**Pale blue edges look like reflections in the glass dome.**

**The saucer shape of the spaceship enables it to do quick U-turns.**

**The glass dome gives the pilot a perfect view.**

**Three engines provide the necessary power for high-speed chases.**

**You could invent alien writing to go on the spaceship.**

**Add rocket-trail colours over the engines while the engine colours are slightly damp. This will allow the tones to blend.**

# Galactic cruiser

Because the distances between galaxies are so great, it would take centuries for a conventional spaceship to travel from one to another. This picture shows an artist's impression of some features that a spaceship would need in order to cruise at speed between galaxies.

**The main shapes**

**Add details such as the engines and the cockpit.**

**Try to keep the spacecraft exactly symmetrical. That is, the right-hand side needs to be a mirror image of the left-hand side.**

**The strong shades of red and blue on the spaceship make it look aggressive.**

**Streamlined wings, for minimum resistance.**

**Turbo engines, to enable the ship to reach hyper-space mode.**

**This ship looks mysterious because you cannot see the pilot through the smoked screen shield.**

**The ship has tough screen shields, to resist any space debris that might hit the ship during its voyage.**

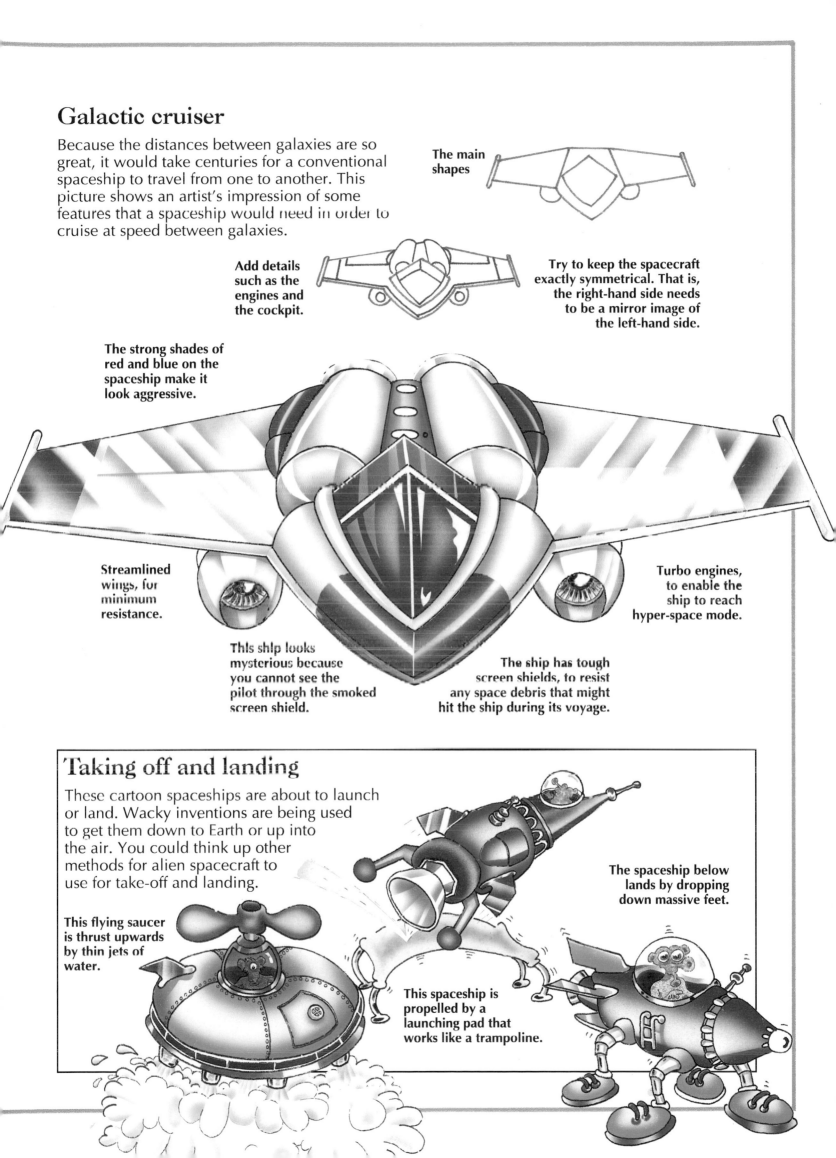

# Taking off and landing

These cartoon spaceships are about to launch or land. Wacky inventions are being used to get them down to Earth or up into the air. You could think up other methods for alien spacecraft to use for take-off and landing.

**This flying saucer is thrust upwards by thin jets of water.**

**The spaceship below lands by dropping down massive feet.**

**This spaceship is propelled by a launching pad that works like a trampoline.**

# Rockets

The first real spaceships were built in the 1950s. By the mid 1960s, a rocket that could take people to the Moon was developed in the USA. It was called a Saturn 5, and is shown on this page. In 1969, a Saturn 5 took people to the Moon for the first time. On the opposite page is a Soyuz rocket, designed in the USSR at around the same time.

## Drawing a Saturn 5

The rocket can be broken down into simple shapes. Use the steps below to help you draw it. Sketch the outlines in pencil first so you get the shapes right.

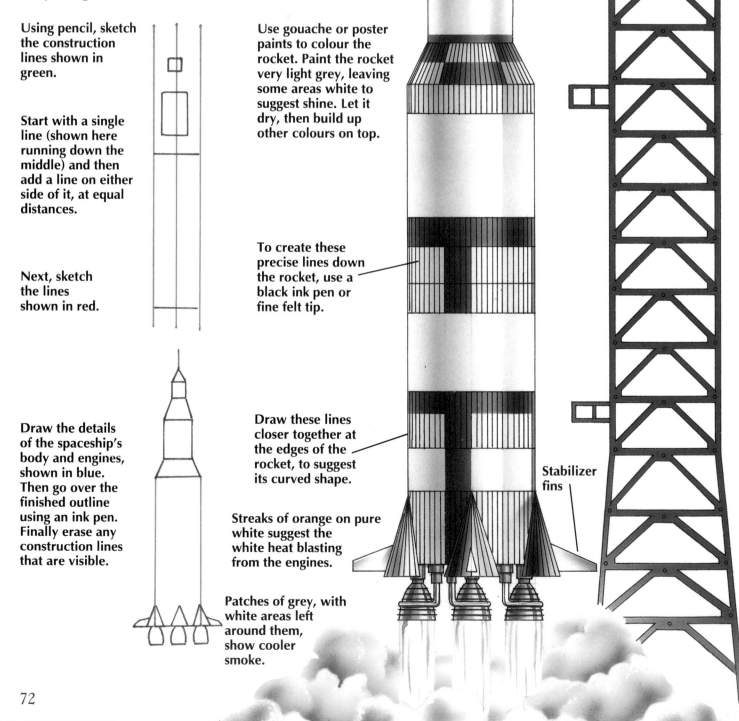

Using pencil, sketch the construction lines shown in green.

Start with a single line (shown here running down the middle) and then add a line on either side of it, at equal distances.

Next, sketch the lines shown in red.

Draw the details of the spaceship's body and engines, shown in blue. Then go over the finished outline using an ink pen. Finally erase any construction lines that are visible.

Use gouache or poster paints to colour the rocket. Paint the rocket very light grey, leaving some areas white to suggest shine. Let it dry, then build up other colours on top.

To create these precise lines down the rocket, use a black ink pen or fine felt tip.

Draw these lines closer together at the edges of the rocket, to suggest its curved shape.

Streaks of orange on pure white suggest the white heat blasting from the engines.

Patches of grey, with white areas left around them, show cooler smoke.

Only this portion of the spaceship comes back to Earth with the astronauts in.

The part of the spaceship that lands on the Moon is held in here.

Launch tower supports rocket before lift-off.

Stabilizer fins

# Drawing a Soyuz rocket

Although a Soyuz rocket looks different from a Saturn 5, it is designed to do a similar job. The first Soyuz rocket was launched by the USSR in 1967. They are still used today, to carry people and satellites into orbit. To draw a Soyuz space rocket, follow these stages.

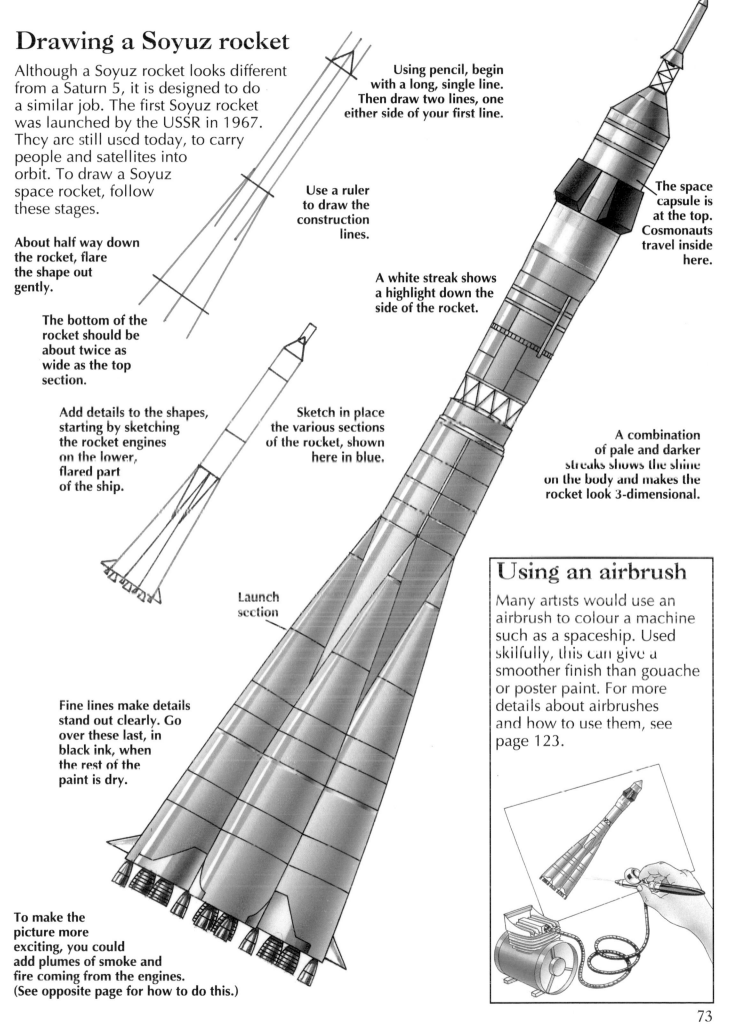

**Using pencil, begin with a long, single line. Then draw two lines, one either side of your first line.**

**Use a ruler to draw the construction lines.**

**About half way down the rocket, flare the shape out gently.**

**The bottom of the rocket should be about twice as wide as the top section.**

**Add details to the shapes, starting by sketching the rocket engines on the lower, flared part of the ship.**

**Sketch in place the various sections of the rocket, shown here in blue.**

**The space capsule is at the top. Cosmonauts travel inside here.**

**A white streak shows a highlight down the side of the rocket.**

**A combination of pale and darker streaks shows the shine on the body and makes the rocket look 3-dimensional.**

**Launch section**

**Fine lines make details stand out clearly. Go over these last, in black ink, when the rest of the paint is dry.**

**To make the picture more exciting, you could add plumes of smoke and fire coming from the engines. (See opposite page for how to do this.)**

## Using an airbrush

Many artists would use an airbrush to colour a machine such as a spaceship. Used skilfully, this can give a smoother finish than gouache or poster paint. For more details about airbrushes and how to use them, see page 123.

73

# The Space Shuttle

The Space Shuttle is the only reusable type of spaceship that has been developed. To blast it clear of the Earth's atmosphere, it has two huge rockets and a giant fuel tank attached to it. When these have been used up, they are detached from the Shuttle and fall back to Earth. The plane-shaped section completes its mission and returns to Earth.

This Shuttle has been drawn using coloured pencils. Loose hatching and ripples of colour give it a stylized, exciting look. (For more information about hatching, see page 122.)

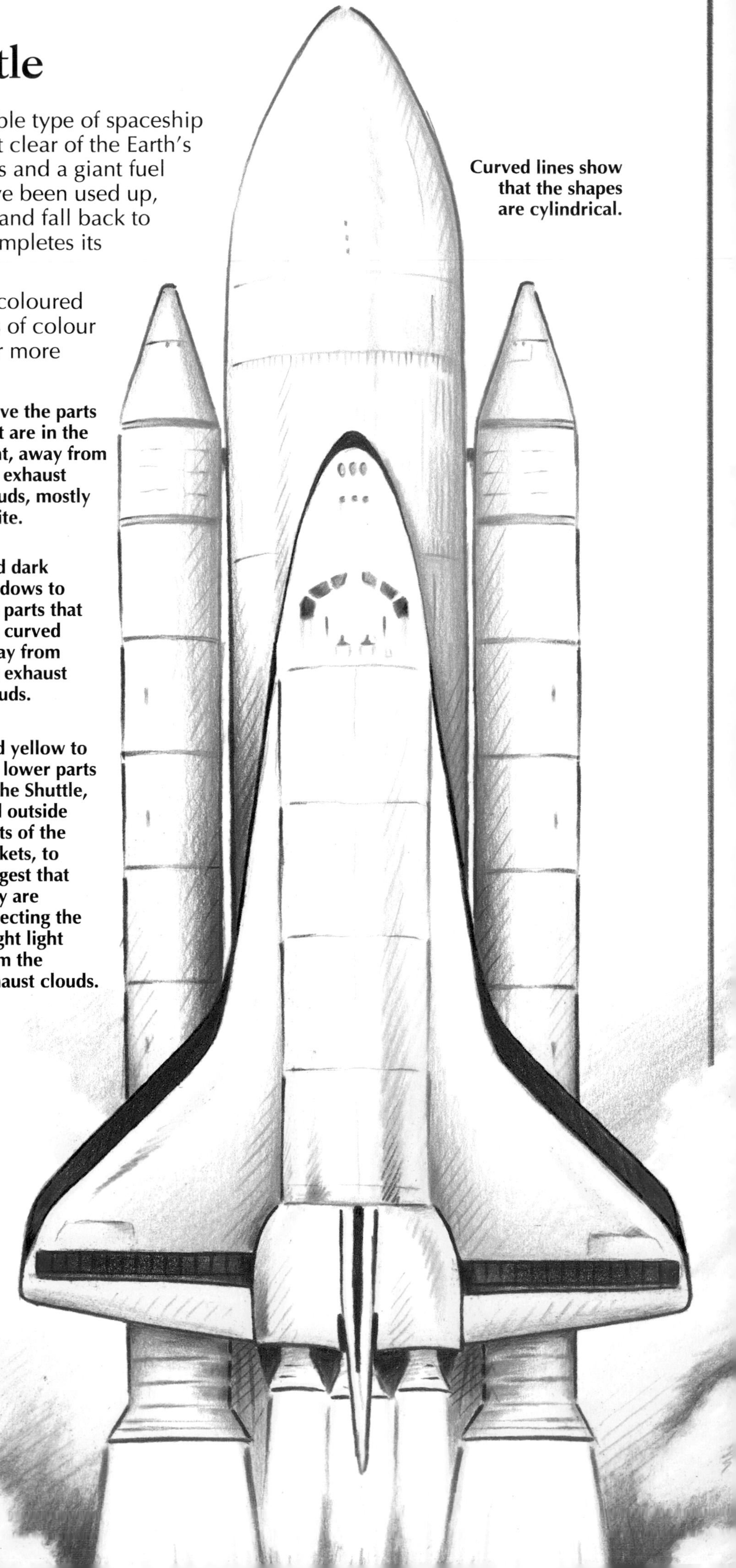

**Curved lines show that the shapes are cylindrical.**

**Sketch the plane-shaped part first (shown in green), then the fuel tank (in the middle), and the two rockets either side (shown in red).**

**Keep the outlines of the shapes symmetrical.**

**Sketch the segments of the rockets and the fuel tank, shown here in blue.**

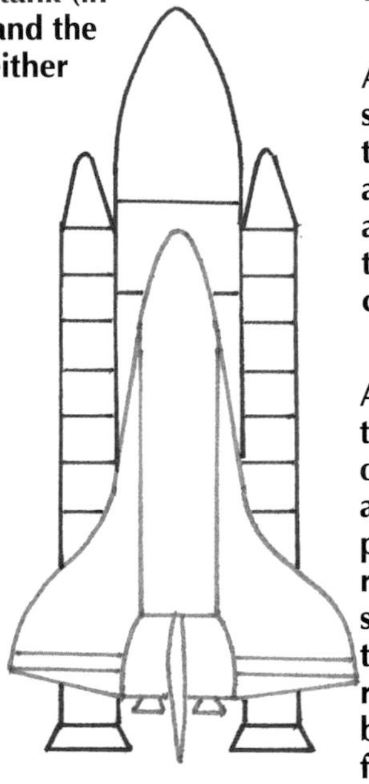

**Leave the parts that are in the light, away from the exhaust clouds, mostly white.**

**Add dark shadows to the parts that are curved away from the exhaust clouds.**

**Add yellow to the lower parts of the Shuttle, and outside parts of the rockets, to suggest that they are reflecting the bright light from the exhaust clouds.**

**Leave space at the bottom of your paper for clouds, exhaust gases and smoke. Use yellow, orange and red to show the various temperatures of the exhaust clouds as they cool.**

# DINOSAURS AND PREHISTORIC LIFE

Millions of years ago, the Earth was inhabited by monster creatures - the dinosaurs - which are scarcely believable today. In this section, you can find out how to draw them, in realistic and cartoon styles. For their full impact, draw them large and paint them vividly. If you like, put something in the picture, such as a tree, to show their giant scale.

Even after the dinosaurs died out, weird looking mammals and birds roamed the Earth. Examples of these are included here, as well as cartoon versions of prehistoric people. These cartoon primitive humans are fairly easy to draw because of their simple clothing and because it does not matter if they look ragged.

# Dinosaur giants

The last dinosaurs died out around 65 million years ago. However, we know what they looked like because their shapes have been preserved. Their markings were not preserved, though, so you can show them with whatever colours you like.

## Diplodocus

These are the rough shapes of the Diplodocus, one of the longest dinosaurs. It measured 27m (89ft) from nose to tail - about as long as a tennis court. Draw the oval body shape first. Then add the long neck and tail.

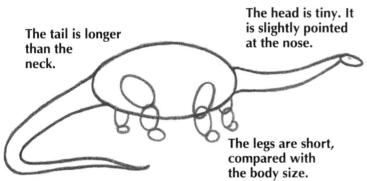

**The tail is longer than the neck.**

**The head is tiny. It is slightly pointed at the nose.**

**The legs are short, compared with the body size.**

**The end of the tail was very thin. It was probably used to whip enemies.**

The Diplodocus had thick, leathery skin, like an elephant's. You could paint it with washes of green watercolour, as shown here.

**When the washes of green watercolour have dried, add darker green ridges all over the body, using a fine brush.**

**Make the ridges shorter on the thinner areas, such as the tail, neck and legs.**

**For highlights on places such as the top of the spine and along the top of the tail, leave the light green wash to show through.**

## Diplodocus model

A simple model, made out of playdough, can be very helpful if you want to make drawings of a Diplodocus from different angles.

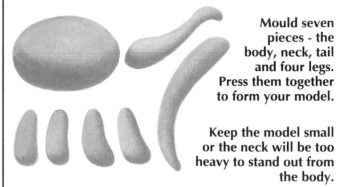

**Mould seven pieces - the body, neck, tail and four legs. Press them together to form your model.**

**Keep the model small or the neck will be too heavy to stand out from the body.**

**Stand the model on some cardboard so that you can move it easily.**

Sketch the shadows that fall on the model. In the finished drawing, the shadows will help to make the animal look solid.

**Colour the far legs a darker shade to emphasize the shadow.**

**Use a darker, thicker mix of the wash colour for the shadows under the body.**

# Stegosaurus

The basic shape of the Stegosaurus is similar to the Diplodocus. However, its neck and tail are slightly shorter in proportion to its body. Also, it has some unique features, which you should include in your initial sketch.

**The head hangs low.**

**The back legs are longer than the front legs.**

**Diamond shaped plates run along the animal's spine.**

**Paint the skin with a light wash. When dry, add a darker layer to the shaded areas.**

**Cover the body with thick white spots. Mix some wash colour with the white to darken the spots in areas of shade.**

**Add a shadow beneath the Stegosaurus, to emphasize its solidity.**

**Use darker shades for the far plates and far legs. This makes them look further away.**

**The spikes on the tail were probably used to injure opponents during fights.**

**Add extra highlights on places such as the side of the body, using tiny flecks of thick white gouache.**

**A long ridge down the neck makes it look solid and muscular.**

## Alternative skins

For warty skin, you could apply the first wash and shadows with watercolour, then dab darker paint all over the body, using a stippling brush.

You can create leathery skin using coloured pencil. Begin with a very light layer of colour, then add darker ridges.

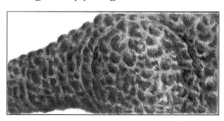

# Cartoon dinosaurs

This cartoon Tyrannosaurus rex (or T. rex) is behaving in a characteristically vicious way. However, because it is a cartoon, it still looks almost harmless. At the bottom of the page, you can see how to paint the cartoon T. rex, using masking fluid and watercolours, to make its skin look bumpy. You can buy masking fluid at art shops.

There are details on how to paint alternative versions of a T. rex on pages 80 and 82.

**Start by sketching the body shape.**

**Add the head shape, then the tail and the limbs.**

**For an aggressive stance, lean the T. rex's body forwards.**

**Frowning eyes make the T. rex look evil.**

**Make the hind legs look solid, so that the T. rex looks powerful and stable.**

**A large tail swishing from side to side makes the dinosaur look powerful and aggressive.**

**To emphasize the leathery texture of the chest and stomach, paint them with different colours from the rest of the body.**

**You could position the front feet so that they look as if they are about to grab a victim. In fact, a real T. rex's front legs and feet were so small that they were useless.**

**Show the far leg under the middle of the T. rex, or else it will look as if it is about to fall over.**

## Painting the skin

Paint on the masking fluid with an old brush. Do not use a new brush, because it will be spoiled for future use with paint.

When the masking fluid is dry, paint the body with several different watercolours. Start with the lightest wash.

When all of the paint is dry, rub off the masking fluid with your fingers. Unpainted patches will be revealed.

**Here, the masking fluid is shown as patches of grey.**

**The paint will not stick to the masking fluid.**

**Decorate the unpainted patches as shown in the big picture above.**

78

# Balancing dinosaurs

A common problem when drawing two-legged dinosaurs is that they can look off-balance. This makes them appear weak. To make them balance, there should be as much weight in front of their legs as behind. Draw a vertical line and build your animal up around it.

**Weight too far back.**

**Weight too far forwards.**

**Vertical line.** Plot the dinosaur around this.

**Show equal amounts of the animal's bulk (including the legs) on either side of the line.**

# Angry Triceratops

The Triceratops was a fierce, plant-eating dinosaur. Its huge, frilled head, three horns and strange beaked mouth help to give it a lot of character. To show one in a very bad mood, give it staring eyes and a downturned mouth.

**Begin by sketching the body shape.**

**Next, sketch the head shape, the frilled crest, the tail and the leg shapes.**

**Use the same technique to paint the Triceratops as used to paint the T. rex.**

**Apply masking fluid to the shapes before you begin painting.**

**Add the facial details and horns to the head shape.**

**Ensure that the Triceratops has a terrible frown.**

**Toes with toe nails make the feet look realistic.**

**Use washes of orange, yellow and brown to paint the markings.**

**Add extra, soft markings with coloured pencils or delicate touches of light watercolours.**

**By showing the sole of one of the front feet the Triceratops will look as if it has one foot in front of the other.**

**Strengthen the shapes of the features with a thin outline of dark grey watercolour.**

79

# Dinosaur characters

By showing dinosaurs as cartoons you can imply that they have individual characters and moods, just like humans. For a funny effect, you can show them with personalities that differ from what is known about them. For example, you could show a vicious T. rex as a timid, nervous individual, like the one on the right.

**Start by sketching the body, then the tail shape.**

**Add the neck and head shape. The head is roughly pear-shaped.**

**The back legs should be large and look powerful.**

**Bulging eye shapes sit on top of the head.**

**Paint the T. rex using the method shown on page 78, with masking fluid and watercolours.**

**An upright body helps make the T. rex look startled.**

**The down-turned mouth and backward-looking eyes give the T. rex a worried expression.**

**Blend the edges of the patches of paint with a little water.**

**When the body colours are dry, go over the outline with dark grey paint, using a brush.**

# Euoplocephalus

Usually, the Euoplocephalus was a peaceful, plant-eating dinosaur. It used its body armour to help protect it from dangerous meat-eaters such as the T. rex. You could show it in a bad mood, about to gain revenge on one of its enemies.

**Sketch a ball shape on the end of the tail, and the bony spikes.**

**The body is squat and powerful-looking.**

**The neck is very short, with a roughly oval-shaped head.**

**The tail has chunks of bone at the end. It is used as a club, to thump enemies.**

**On top of a pale mauve wash, build up slightly darker shades to show the shape of the dinosaur's armour-plating.**

**A streak of yellow on each spike makes it look like tough bone.**

**Yellow eyes exaggerate the look of anger on the dinosaur's face.**

**The frowning eyes and down-turned mouth make the Euoplocephalus look very angry.**

80

# Parasaurolophus

The Parasaurolophus was a very fast runner, so you could show one in a pose that makes it look athletic. It could look arrogant, because it is confident that it can outrun any dinosaur that tries to catch it.

The body is tilted forwards, to exaggerate the sense of movement.

Parasaurolophus could blow through its long crest to make loud trumpeting noises.

The trailing tail emphasizes the speed of the dinosaur.

Closed eyes and a faint smile make the Parasaurolophus look arrogant.

Add darker patches of paint while the light washes are damp.

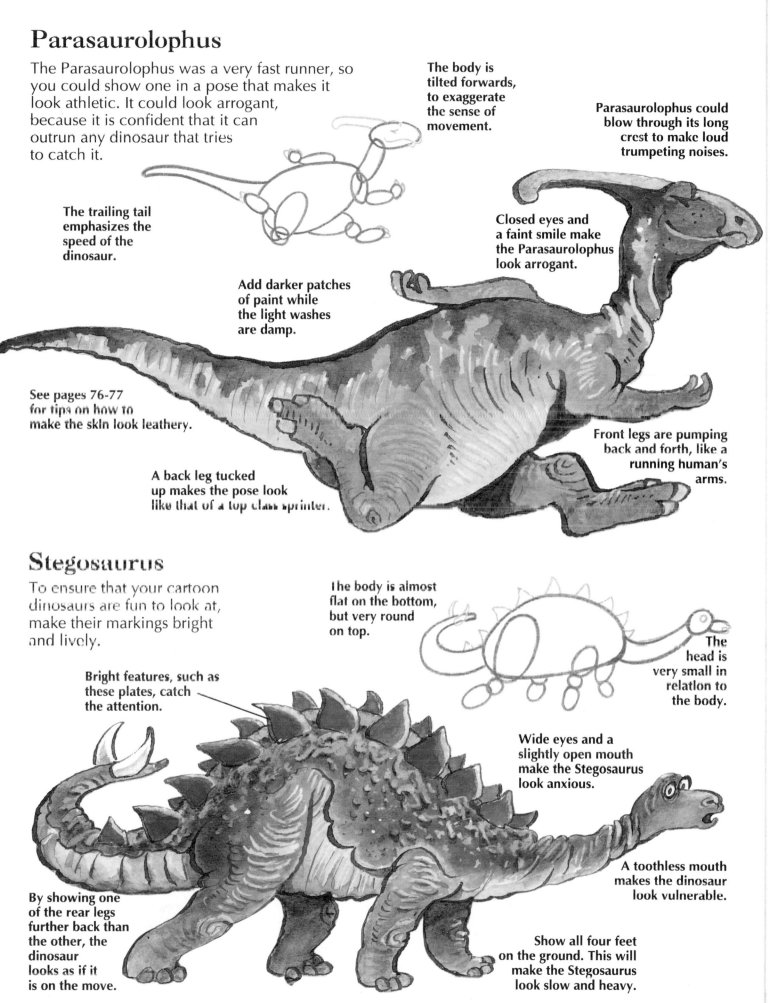

See pages 76-77 for tips on how to make the skin look leathery.

Front legs are pumping back and forth, like a running human's arms.

A back leg tucked up makes the pose look like that of a top class sprinter.

# Stegosaurus

To ensure that your cartoon dinosaurs are fun to look at, make their markings bright and lively.

The body is almost flat on the bottom, but very round on top.

The head is very small in relation to the body.

Bright features, such as these plates, catch the attention.

Wide eyes and a slightly open mouth make the Stegosaurus look anxious.

A toothless mouth makes the dinosaur look vulnerable.

By showing one of the rear legs further back than the other, the dinosaur looks as if it is on the move.

Show all four feet on the ground. This will make the Stegosaurus look slow and heavy.

# Tyrannosaurus rex

With an orange-eyed frown and a huge mouth exposing dagger-like teeth, this drawing gives an idea of how terrifying a real Tyrannosaurus rex would have been. To make this dinosaur look even more horrific, you could draw it so that it looks as if it is attacking you.

**Start by sketching the body, tail and head shapes, shown in red.**

**Add the shapes of the limbs, shown in blue. Then sketch the facial features, along with the claws.**

**Add warts by drawing individual, scaly looking blobs using coloured pencils.**

**Light shadows on the body help to define the shapes of the muscles.**

**To make the leathery ridges look solid add regular, dark, curved shadows.**

**On this picture, watercolour has been applied on the far leg and some of the ridges of the tail, to soften the shadows.**

**The T. rex's skin is warty in places and leathery in others.**

**Begin colouring the skin by applying light layers of the base colours.**

**Remember that you can make your T. Rex any colour you like, because nobody knows for certain what the dinosaurs' markings were like.**

**The shading on the leathery part of the body was made by cross hatching. For more information see page 122.**

**T. rex's front legs were withered and almost useless.**

**Add dark shadows on places such as the lower belly.**

**The feet look like those of a giant chicken.**

# Compsognathus

Compsognathuses were about as big as turkeys. They hunted in packs. By drawing several of them, based on the one shown here, you could create your own pack of vicious little dinosaurs.

**The large tail was used to help the Compsognathus to balance.**

**The body is held almost parallel to the ground.**

**The Compsognathus was fast and agile, using its nimble legs to dash about.**

# Flying creatures

The Pteranodon, shown here, was a reptile that could fly. Each of its wings was about as long as two people lying end to end. Its wings were covered in skin, like a bat's.

**Draw a faint dotted line and use this to position the body, legs and arms.**

**For highlights, use a thick mix of light fawn.**

**The head had a huge crest on top.**

**Add the wings to the arm shapes.**

**Paint the Pteranodon with a thin grey wash of watercolour. When dry, go over it with a thin pinkish brown wash.**

**At the ends of the arms were three short fingers and one long one. The wing was joined to the long finger.**

**Add shadows and veins in dark brown.**

**If you like, you could make your Pteranodon more vivid than the one shown here.**

# Archaeopteryx

The Archaeopteryx was probably the first bird. It was not good at flying because it was too heavy. Many scientists think that it climbed trees, threw itself off and simply glided in the air. You could draw one doing this.

By showing it in a cartoon style, with wide eyes and a manic grin, you could suggest that it is excited at having managed to fly, or perhaps it is out of control and is about to crash.

**Using an ink pen, go over the Archaeopteryx's outline, plus the feather tips on the wings and tail.**

**Colour the bird with felt tips.**

**Give the Archaeopteryx large bulging eyes and fill its mouth with teeth.**

**Start by sketching the relatively small body. Then add the large head, long tail and the wings.**

**Sketch the shape of the feathers.**

**Like the Pteranodon, the Archaeopteryx had fingers.**

**Allow the different shades to touch. This will cause them to bleed into one another, giving a soft, blurred effect.**

# Other prehistoric creatures

There were plenty of other weird prehistoric animals, besides the ones that have appeared on the last few pages. Some examples, plus guides to drawing them, appear here.

On a Parasaurolophus, the crest is longer than the head.

Paint patches of green and light blue, to create a mottled, slimy-looking skin.

## Crested dinosaurs

Dinosaurs that had crests on their heads are called hadrosaurs. To emphasize the striking shapes of the crests, colour them brightly.

You could show the dinosaur's crest with markings that look like any modern animal's. This Lambeosaurus's crest has been given markings like a giraffe.

For a Corythosaurus, sketch the head shape first.

Add warts and loose shapes under the chin.

Add the crest shape by drawing a large circle near the top of the head.

## Diatryma

The Diatryma was a massive bird-like creature, which was nearly as tall as an African elephant.

Balance line

Make sure that half of the body's bulk lies on each side of the balance line.

For the feathers, paint a mixture of mid-blue, white and dark blue over the base washes. Apply the paint with short flicks of the brush in one direction only.

Add occasional strokes of black to darken the feathers, especially in shadowy areas.

For the base wash use light blue. When dry, add another layer to the underside for shadows.

Use washes of grey on the end of the beak. Leave highlights white, to make the beak look shiny.

Apply a light fawn wash to the legs. When it is dry, add details, using a sharpened brown pencil.

# Woolly rhinoceros

The woolly rhinoceros looked similar to a modern rhino, except that it was covered in thick fur.

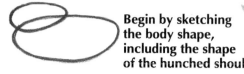

Begin by sketching the body shape, including the shape of the hunched shoulders.

Add the legs and the head to the body shapes.

A white glint in the eye makes the rhino look mean.

Use dark grey on a light grey wash for the wrinkly skin.

A raised leg makes the woolly rhino look as if it might be about to charge.

Use a light yellowish brown wash on the body. Build up the woolly coat by using short brush strokes of dark brown.

Add black using short brush strokes for extra shadows.

# Smilodon

This sabre-toothed cat, called a Smilodon, ate other large mammals, such as deer. You can bring it to life by showing it pouncing.

Sketch the body shape first, then add the head and the leg shapes.

Erase the body parts that are obscured by other parts, before you begin colouring.

Sketch the huge mouth and teeth before painting.

Paint a light yellowish brown base wash on all parts except the face and the chest.

Show darkest areas of fur, and shadows, using dark grey.

Make the fur look realistic by adding short brush strokes of light brown.

# Make your own monster

You could try mixing up some of the heads, tails and bodies on these pages to make your own imaginary monster. For a more life-like monster than the cartoon creature shown here, draw your monster in a realistic style.

# Prehistoric people

Prehistoric people began living on Earth about 2 million years ago, more than 60 million years after the dinosaurs died out. For amusing pictures, you could draw prehistoric people as a family of cartoon cave dwellers. Because you can put cartoon characters into all sorts of impossible situations, you could even shown them side by side with dinosaurs.

**Use the same basic shape for the man and the woman.**

**Draw the outlines of the clothes, hair and beard with a felt tip or an ink pen.**

**Use a brown felt tip for the spots on the clothing. Then shade the rest of the clothing using a yellow felt tip.**

**By applying the felt tips quickly you can create a haphazard effect. This adds to the rough look of these primitive people.**

**Add hairy arms and legs with a pencil.**

**A touch of grey on the lower edge of the axe head makes the axe look more solid.**

**You can create a tooth necklace with just a few jagged lines.**

## Children

To draw boys and girls, sketch pear-shaped bodies. Also, give them thinner arms and legs than for adults.

**For the girl's clothes, add a jagged-hemmed skirt to the bottom of the pear-shaped body.**

**For a baby, make the head large in proportion to the rest of the body.**

**Add a bone in the hair, to give the baby a cute look.**

**Large ears**

**Body details, such as the legs, arms and feet, can be drawn very sketchily.**

## Turning around

Using tracing paper, you can turn characters around. Trace the figure and simply turn the tracing over for the opposite view. Some features must be redrawn, to make the picture correct. For example, if your character has clothes off one shoulder or a club in one hand, this has to be reversed again.

86

# MACHINES

Most of the next section is devoted to
how to draw cars, trucks, trains, planes and
boats. There are some useful techniques included,
such as how to give the impression of something
under water and how to do exploded drawings
which show the way in which parts
of a machine fit together.

This sort of drawing is fairly technical but
there are opportunities for using your imagination.
For instance, you can decorate, or customize,
the cars you draw, or devise cartoons
of motorbikes and their riders.

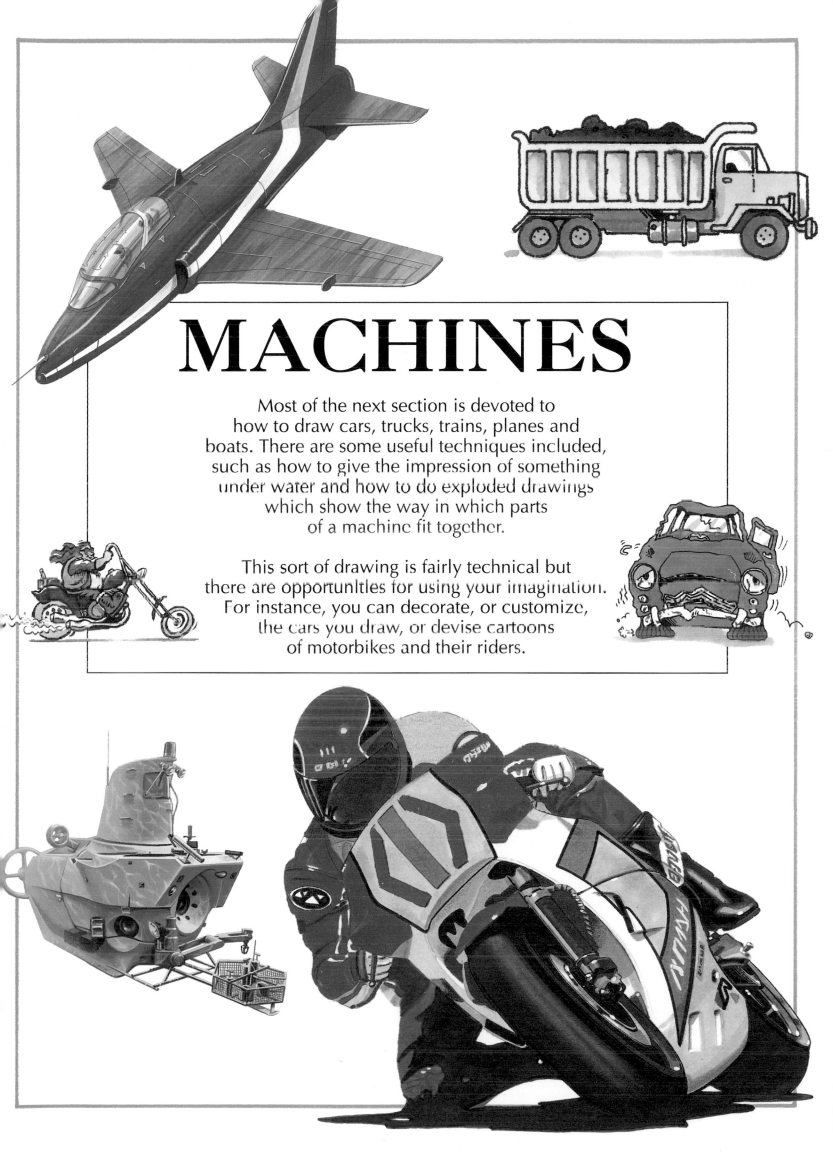

# Cars

The basic shapes of cars are fairly simple. The tricky thing is to get the perspective right and make the car symmetrical. A car is roughly made up of a box shape, with four circles near the corners, and a smaller, flatter box on top. By varying the proportions of these shapes, you can create different types of car, from an upright vintage car through to a sleek, low-slung sports car.

Some people customize cars as a hobby, decorating them with their own paintwork. You could create some original designs, such as those on the right.

**Haphazard blobs create a wacky paint job.**

**For this car, put yellow down first, then add green and red when it is dry.**

**For this flaming speedster, apply yellow first, let it dry, then add the red on top.**

## Vintage car

This vintage car is based on a 1911 Vauxhall Prince Henry. Its body panels are shown as simple blocks of colour. Use bright felt tips for a bold, stylized picture like this.

**Sketch the outline of the car, copying the lines in blue first, then the green, then the red.**

**Outline each shape with a thin black line, to make it stand out.**

**There are no shadows on this picture, but the angles in the body, especially at the front, give it shape.**

**This eye-catching style would be ideal on a poster.**

**Include details such as the horn, headlights and spare wheel.**

## Drawing a wheel

To show a wheel at an angle, draw an oval shape on the side of the car body. Then draw a smaller oval inside it, for the wheel hub. Next, erase any parts of the ovals that go over the car body. Then draw in the front edge of the wheel and shade it in.

**Draw a curve to show the inside edge of the wheel hub.**

**Erase the dotted line.**

**Shade in the gap behind the wheel.**

**Front edge**

# Exploded drawing

The sports car below is shown as an exploded drawing. The technique is used by designers to show how the different parts of a machine fit together, by drawing them hovering near their true position. By showing parts lifted away from the main body of the car, you can show areas that would otherwise be hidden.

To sketch the picture, follow the steps on the right. Below are tips on how to finish the picture, with some ideas for variations on it.

**For the body shape, start by sketching the blue boxes. Build up the car shape, shown in red, inside the blue lines.**

**Draw the parts near where they are supposed to fit on the car.**

**Arrows show where parts are supposed to slot in.**

**You could remove other parts, such as a door, or reveal the engine (although you would need to look at a real engine, or a picture of one, to get the details correct).**

**This car was painted with an airbrush. You can also achieve good results using marker pens. For details of both methods see page 123.**

# Crazy cartoon cars

If you let your imagination run wild, you can turn just about any object into a car, as shown on the right. You can also show cars that are altered so that they take on human characteristics. Headlights can become eyes, while radiator grilles can become mouths.

**Bright eyes, a grinning mouth and bright colours characterize this friendly car.**

**Sharp shapes, big wheels, narrow eyes and bared teeth show a fierce car.**

**This worn out car has tired eyes and a down-turned mouth, to match its battered body.**

# Tractors, trucks, trains and planes

Big vehicles, such as tractors and trucks, are made up of large, solid shapes that are easy to sketch. For a farm tractor such as the one shown here, start with the shapes shown in red. Add very large wheels at the back and smaller wheels at the front.

**The height of the cab is about the same as the depth of the tractor body.**

**The body is deep, to hold the engine.**

**The back wheels are about one and a half times as big as the front wheels.**

**In this simple drawing, the windows have been left unpainted. You could add a glassy sheen to them - see the trucks below.**

Exhaust pipe

**The engine is partly exposed.**

**On farm vehicles, tyres have deep treads, so that they can grip in muddy conditions. Show the treads with slanting lines around the edge.**

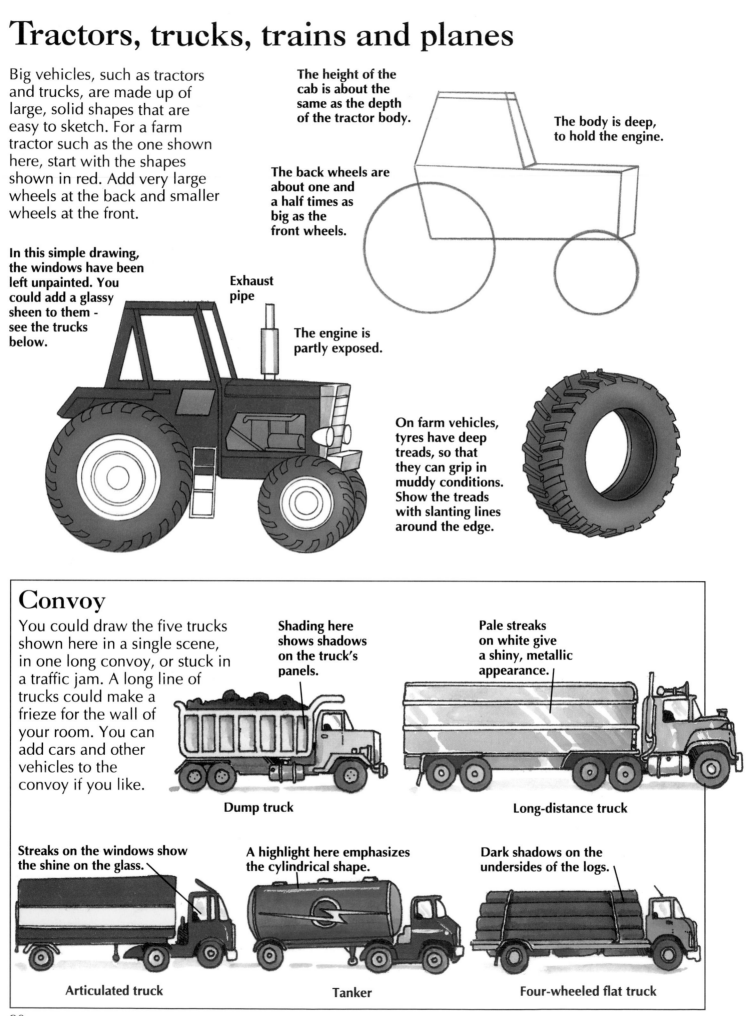

## Convoy

You could draw the five trucks shown here in a single scene, in one long convoy, or stuck in a traffic jam. A long line of trucks could make a frieze for the wall of your room. You can add cars and other vehicles to the convoy if you like.

**Shading here shows shadows on the truck's panels.**

Dump truck

**Pale streaks on white give a shiny, metallic appearance.**

Long-distance truck

**Streaks on the windows show the shine on the glass.**

Articulated truck

**A highlight here emphasizes the cylindrical shape.**

Tanker

**Dark shadows on the undersides of the logs.**

Four-wheeled flat truck

# Steam train

To draw this old steam train, begin by sketching a cylinder. Then sketch a shallow box beneath the cylinder, and a more upright box behind it. Sketch some ovals to show wheels at an angle.

**Use felt tips to create a bright, toy-like effect.**

**Driver's cab**

**Iron wheels have thick spokes.**

**Shade the cylinder with curved lines to make it look rounded.**

**Connecting rod enables one wheel to drive another.**

**Draw two long strips for tracks, with planks under them.**

# Jet planes

To sketch a jet plane, start with the shape shown in red. Then add the wings shown in blue, and the tail shown in green. Paint the body with a light wash of orange. When this is dry, add darker orange to show areas in shadow. Applying the paint in streaks from front to back emphasizes the direction and speed of the plane's travel.

**This plane is based on a jet called a Hawk.**

**Exhaust outlet**

**Using a very fine ink pen add fine lines on the body of the plane, to show the flaps on its tail and wings.**

**Use streaks of bluish grey to show the surface of the cockpit.**

**Show highlights on the plane by adding thin streaks of white gouache.**

**Curved lines across the body of the plane show its sections and emphasize its curved shape.**

# Formation flying

To draw a flying team, repeat the outline shown below, in any formation you like. Add trails of different coloured smoke behind the planes.

**Show all the planes in the team with the same colour.**

**Draw smoke trails using a series of curves, like these.**

**If you show a plane from below, do not show this part of the tail.**

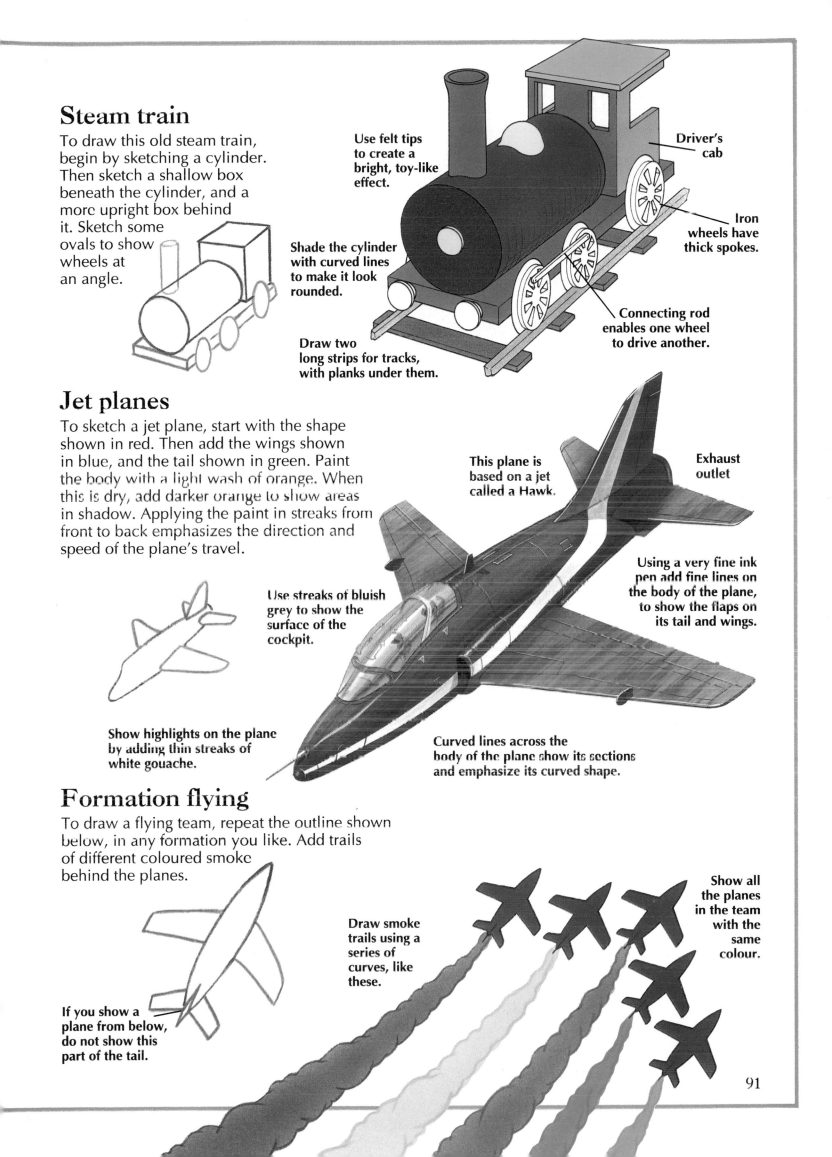

# Bikes

This early bicycle was called a penny farthing. It did not have a chain or any gears. Instead, the pedals turned the front wheels directly. Its huge front wheel meant that the distance covered during each rotation of the pedals was very big.

To give the penny farthing an old look, paint it with watercolours and gouache or poster paints. Use dull colours, such as greys and browns.

**Apply lightest shades first. When these are dry, add darker colours.**

**Add highlights using white gouache or poster paint, applied with a fine brush.**

**Add the spokes last, using a fine ink pen and a ruler.**

Below are examples of two modern bikes, with tips on how to draw and colour them. The violet bike is a racing bike, while the one below it is a mountain bike. Both have been painted using an airbrush (see page 123), to make the paintwork look very smooth.

**By drawing the bikes larger than shown here, you will be able to show their close details.**

**Show the chain as a series of tiny touching circles, using a fine ink pen.**

**Use dark grey for the wheels. A fine ink pen emphasizes the chunky treads.**

**You could show bikes with two-tone paint jobs.**

## Drawing a bicycle

Draw two wheels of equal size, about half a wheel's diameter apart. Then sketch the frame shown in blue, and the parts shown in green.

Leave pale streaks on the frame to make it look shiny. Use streaks of grey for the chrome areas. Finally, paint the tyres black.

**Add spokes with a black ink pen.**

# A motorbike

To capture the speed and power of a motorbike, draw the picture at a moment of high drama, such as when the rider steers the bike around a tight corner. Motorbike magazines contain exciting photographs of the latest machinery in action, which you can use for inspiration and reference.

**Start by sketching ovals for the two wheels. Then add the rough shapes of the bike, shown in red.**

**Use felt tips or marker pens to give results like this.**

**The rider and bike are tricky to draw because the shapes are foreshortened. See page 121 for help with this.**

**Next, sketch the rider's body shapes.**

**Create flashes of bright highlight using blobs of white gouache, or white correcting fluid.**

**Shades of grey on the bike's body help to make it look solid.**

**Apply light colours first. Add extra layers of colour to areas that are in shadow.**

**A soft streak of chalk, blended in with your finger, shows the curve of the wheel.**

**Solid black shows the darkest shadows.**

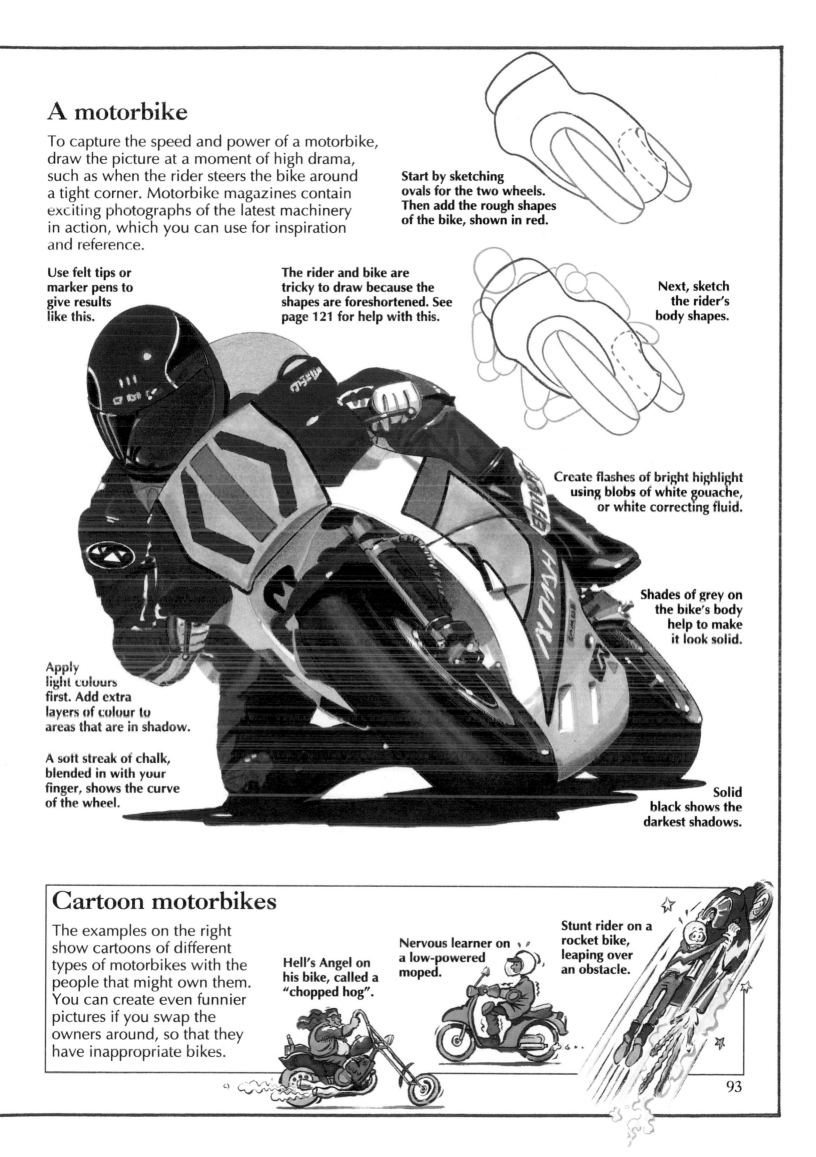

# Cartoon motorbikes

The examples on the right show cartoons of different types of motorbikes with the people that might own them. You can create even funnier pictures if you swap the owners around, so that they have inappropriate bikes.

**Hell's Angel on his bike, called a "chopped hog".**

**Nervous learner on a low-powered moped.**

**Stunt rider on a rocket bike, leaping over an obstacle.**

# Sea vehicles

This lifeboat is designed to be stable so that it will not capsize in stormy seas. Also, it is fast-moving so that it can reach the scene of an accident quickly.

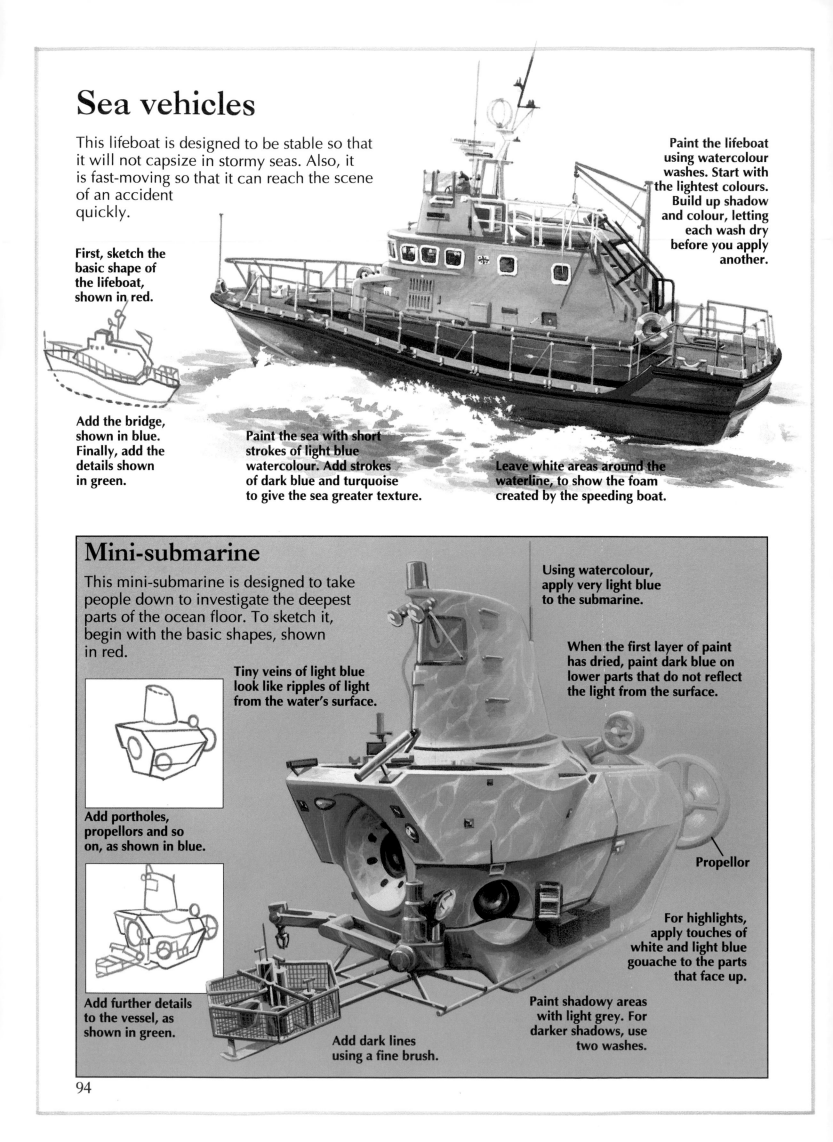

Paint the lifeboat using watercolour washes. Start with the lightest colours. Build up shadow and colour, letting each wash dry before you apply another.

First, sketch the basic shape of the lifeboat, shown in red.

Add the bridge, shown in blue. Finally, add the details shown in green.

Paint the sea with short strokes of light blue watercolour. Add strokes of dark blue and turquoise to give the sea greater texture.

Leave white areas around the waterline, to show the foam created by the speeding boat.

## Mini-submarine

This mini-submarine is designed to take people down to investigate the deepest parts of the ocean floor. To sketch it, begin with the basic shapes, shown in red.

Using watercolour, apply very light blue to the submarine.

When the first layer of paint has dried, paint dark blue on lower parts that do not reflect the light from the surface.

Tiny veins of light blue look like ripples of light from the water's surface.

Add portholes, propellors and so on, as shown in blue.

Add further details to the vessel, as shown in green.

Propellor

For highlights, apply touches of white and light blue gouache to the parts that face up.

Add dark lines using a fine brush.

Paint shadowy areas with light grey. For darker shadows, use two washes.

# BUILDINGS

Drawing buildings is a good way to improve your general drawing skills. You could take a sketchbook with you when you go out and draw details such as interesting doors and windows. Drawing the front and side of a building will help you practise showing things in the correct proportion and perspective. The technique of drawing things in perspective is explained on pages 120-121.

Pictures of buildings can look very dramatic if you draw them from an unusual perspective. For instance, you could draw skyscrapers from high above, with tiny cars in the street far below. A building drawn from ground level, on the other hand, can look imposing and overwhelming.

# A fairytale castle

Fairytale castles are fun to create, because you can draw them with exaggerated details, such as long, thin towers topped with pointed roofs. For a dreamy effect, you can leave out realistic details such as stonework and tiles. To complete the fantasy scene, place your castle at the top of an impossibly high, narrow mountain.

**Giant banners fluttering in the breeze show that the king is at home.**

**Use watercolours mixed with lots of water. This will give the picture a soft, misty feel, and will make it look magical.**

**The outlines, windows and other details can look a little haphazard and unreal.**

**Inside the iron gate, or portcullis, it is dark and mysterious.**

**Paint very soft, flat shadows on walls facing away from the sun.**

## Sketching the castle

When sketching the basic shapes, make the castle look wider towards the top than the bottom. Make the towers lean slightly outwards, to emphasize the height and precariousness of the castle.

**The sun is shining from this side of the castle. Leave the walls facing the sun pure white.**

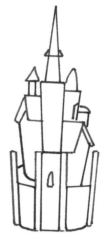

Next, add turrets at the tops of the towers and other details such as spiralling staircases, arched windows and a gate. Draw the details freehand, so that the picture has a casual, rather than formal, feel.

**The lowered drawbridge and raised portcullis make the castle look less forbidding than if they were closed.**

# A haunted house

An abandoned, derelict house can be made to look creepy if you show it with ramshackle walls and gaping holes in the roof. Bats, a strange shadow inside an eerily-lit window and angular, dark trees will add to the spooky atmosphere of your picture. If you add ghostly shapes swooping around the house, and a flash of lightning, you will make it look even more terrifying.

**Start by sketching the basic shape of the house. Draw the walls so that they slope towards one another as they approach the top. This emphasizes the forbidding size of the house, and gives a dramatic look to the picture.**

**Add the windows, doors, turrets and the pointed sections of roof. Draw these lines faintly, using a ruler. You can use these straight lines as guidelines when you produce a more random, tumbledown look at a later stage.**

**Finally, sketch the steps and balcony at the front of the house. Then, in pencil, draw the details of the house, such as the stonework, slates, wood panelling and windows. Finally, go over the details with a fine ink pen.**

**For missing slates, leave some black holes. Draw some loose planks hanging down over the others.**

**Use a variety of shades of blue, to make the house look as if it is bathed in moonlight.**

**A strange light at a window suggests a ghostly presence. Fill half the window with shadow, in a vaguely human shape.**

**Paint the house with light washes of watercolour. The inked details will show through the paint.**

**Moonlight casts cold shadows on the house and suggests a menacing atmosphere.**

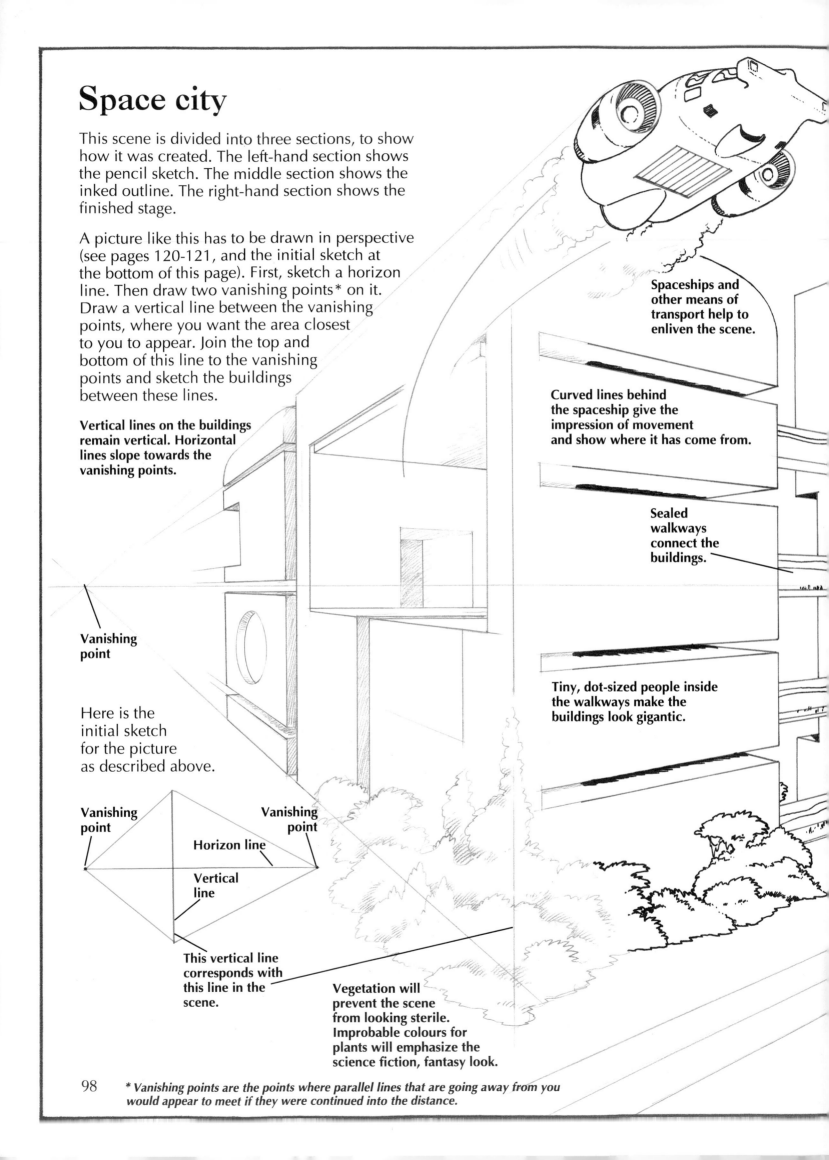

# Space city

This scene is divided into three sections, to show how it was created. The left-hand section shows the pencil sketch. The middle section shows the inked outline. The right-hand section shows the finished stage.

A picture like this has to be drawn in perspective (see pages 120-121, and the initial sketch at the bottom of this page). First, sketch a horizon line. Then draw two vanishing points* on it. Draw a vertical line between the vanishing points, where you want the area closest to you to appear. Join the top and bottom of this line to the vanishing points and sketch the buildings between these lines.

**Vertical lines on the buildings remain vertical. Horizontal lines slope towards the vanishing points.**

**Vanishing point**

Here is the initial sketch for the picture as described above.

**Vanishing point**

**Vanishing point**

**Horizon line**

**Vertical line**

**This vertical line corresponds with this line in the scene.**

**Vegetation will prevent the scene from looking sterile. Improbable colours for plants will emphasize the science fiction, fantasy look.**

**Spaceships and other means of transport help to enliven the scene.**

**Curved lines behind the spaceship give the impression of movement and show where it has come from.**

**Sealed walkways connect the buildings.**

**Tiny, dot-sized people inside the walkways make the buildings look gigantic.**

*Vanishing points are the points where parallel lines that are going away from you would appear to meet if they were continued into the distance.*

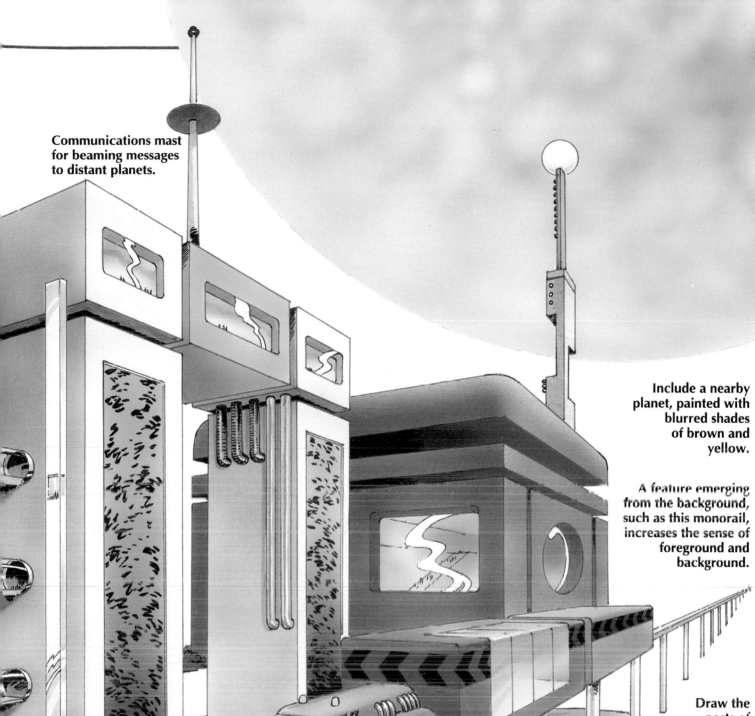

**Communications mast for beaming messages to distant planets.**

**Include a nearby planet, painted with blurred shades of brown and yellow.**

**A feature emerging from the background, such as this monorail, increases the sense of foreground and background.**

**Draw the posts of the monorail closer together as they recede into the background.**

**This scene was painted with an airbrush, to give a smooth, regular look to the picture.**

# Highlights and shadows

Objects with shiny finishes, such as windows and metal sheets, can have obvious highlights. To draw convincing shadows and highlights, you need to imagine the shape of the object and where the light will fall on it.

**Flat surfaces, such as windows, can have zig-zagged areas of highlight.**

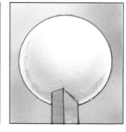

**Add shadows to a curved surface using soft, curved strokes of colour.**

99

# Amazing architecture

Some real buildings, like the two shown here, would not look out of place in science fiction movies. To make an impressive picture of a building, it is important to show it from an angle which emphasizes its design. However, a building such as the Sydney Opera House in Australia is so unusual that it looks stunning from any angle.

In this drawing, a spectacular sunset completes the scene. Concentrate on finishing the Opera House first, before you add the sky.

**Start by sketching the foundations, shown here in red.**

**Sketch the roof sections, shown in blue, on the foundations. Sketch the shapes shown in green last.**

**For the sunset, paint a wash of light yellow ink or watercolour over the whole sky. Deepen some parts with a second wash while the first is still damp.**

**To complete the sky, add light tones of red and orange to the scene.**

**Using coloured pencil, put a very light, soft shade of grey all over the roof.**

The roof sections of the Opera House are designed to look like gigantic billowing sails on an old ship. They are covered with shiny white ceramic tiles. This gives them a bright, clean appearance.

**Show the darkest shadows with pure black ink or watercolour. For lighter shadows, apply grey washes.**

# The Chrysler Building

The Chrysler Building is in New York, USA. It is a perfect example of a design style called Art Deco, which was popular in the 1920s and 30s. By drawing the building from an extremely high angle, called a bird's eye view, you can emphasize its height. In fact, when it was built, the Chrysler Building was the tallest building in the world.

**To sketch the building in perspective \*, first plot a vanishing point on your paper, then draw a line up from it (shown here as a broken line).**

**Next, roughly sketch a diamond shape, with the broken line going through its middle. Then sketch lines going from each of the diamond's corners to the vanishing point.**

**Add another diamond, with edges parallel to the first diamond.**

**Vanishing point**

**Draw the shape of the curved section on top of the building. Each of its curves should end at a point on the broken line.**

**Add details to the building, using the lines that you have already sketched for guidance.**

**Erase the sketched guide lines that you no longer need.**

**Go over the outlines of the building and its details (including the windows) with an ink pen.**

*\*There is more about perspective on pages 120-121.*

**Paint the building with light fawn washes, to make it look as if it is bathed in warm evening sunshine.**

The building contains typical Art Deco features such as symmetrical shapes and decorative arches. Also, it is made from shiny materials such as metals and lots of polished stone.

**Show shadows using light grey, and extreme highlights with touches of thick white gouache.**

101

# Bad mood building

For an amusing drawing, you could show a building as a cartoon. An appropriate character for a skyscraper might be that of a bad-tempered monster. In the scene shown here, a lightning bolt has hit a skyscraper's transmitter mast, bringing it to life. The building is stomping through town like a concrete King Kong.

**The windows have been converted into frowning eyes.**

**Jagged lines around the fist exaggerate the force of its punches.**

**Details, such as the street lamp in the building's fist, make the scene vivid and interesting.**

**Giant arms give the building a human-like appearance.**

**Other buildings are suffering the consequences of the building's vile temper.**

**The building has even grown giant feet, complete with boots, so that it can go on its wrecking spree.**

You can show cartoon buildings in any situation you like. For example, these buildings are dancing.

**Movement lines emphasize the action of the buildings.**

## Factory monster

Cartoon techniques can be used to make a serious point. In this drawing, a chemical factory has been made into a monster, spouting pollution from its mouth.

**Dingy colours help to convey the grim message of the cartoon.**

102

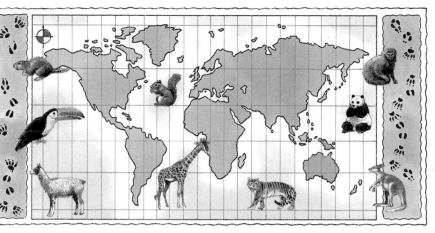

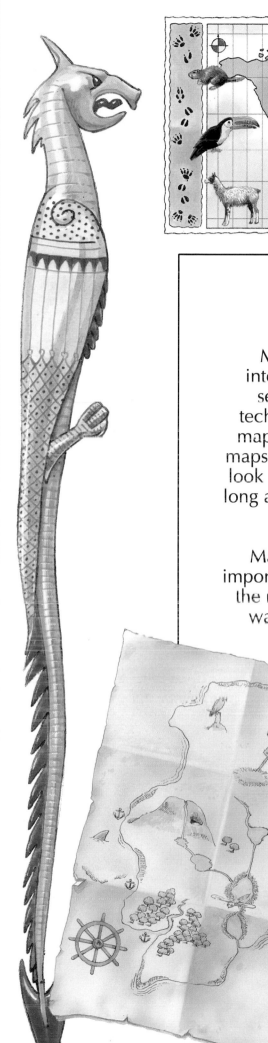

# MAPS

Maps provide a lot of scope for interesting, detailed drawings. This section of the book explains the techniques needed to draw a proper map with symbols, as well as fantasy maps of imaginary areas, and maps that look as if they were drawn and painted long ago. You can also see how to make a game based on a map.

Maps have a practical use, so it is important that they are clear to read. On the next few pages you can see some ways in which to make them look decorative, as well.

# World and country maps

All world maps are distorted, because it is impossible to show the whole of the Earth's curve accurately on a flat map. Views of the world that are flat are called projections. The two projections on the right were created over a hundred years ago.

You can show different sorts of information on a world map. The map below shows pictures of animals, and indicates where they come from. If you want to draw this map, you can see how to enlarge it at the bottom of the page. The animals were drawn separately and then cut out and stuck on the map.

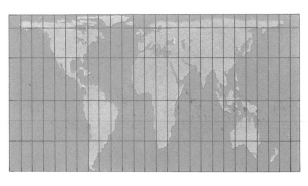

In this projection, the sizes of areas of land are correct in relation to each other. However, the shape of most of the land is distorted a lot.

This projection is useful for giving an idea of the shapes of areas of land. It is not accurate for showing the relative sizes of areas of land.

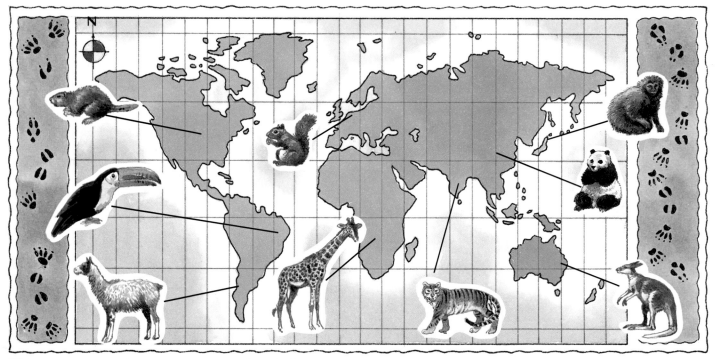

## How to enlarge the wildlife map

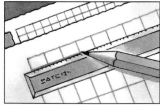

Copy the grid of lines (called lines of latitude and longitude) from the finished map above. Space them twice as far apart.

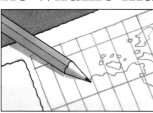

The lines will form a large grid of different-sized boxes. Now copy the map above box by box into your grid, in pencil.

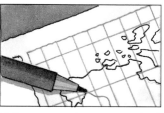

When you have copied the map, draw over the outlines of the landforms with a pen to make them more permanent.

Decorate the map and add a compass point to show where north is. You could add a patterned border and other pictures.

# Hi-tech mapping

Mapmakers (called cartographers) have a range of accurate devices which they use to record map details. For example, they use satellites to plot extremely accurate maps of landforms. The satellite image on the right shows clouds over part of Europe. The curled cloud is a severe storm located over the British Isles. Images of this kind are used to create reliable maps showing weather patterns.

# Picture from space

Satellite photos of places in darkness can show towns picked out as clusters of lights. To draw a picture in this style, use thick white poster paint or gouache on black paper. Base your picture on a map of a country, taken from an atlas.

**Using an atlas, trace the outline of the country you want to draw, in pencil. Mark the positions of towns with dots. This map shows Sicily, an Italian island.**

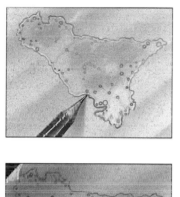

**Put the tracing on top of some black paper and draw over the outline of the country and the positions of towns with a sharp pencil, to press them into the paper.**

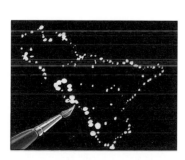

**Using thick white paint, mark the towns and cities on the map with clusters of small dots. Dab the paint on the paper with the tip of a fine-pointed brush.**

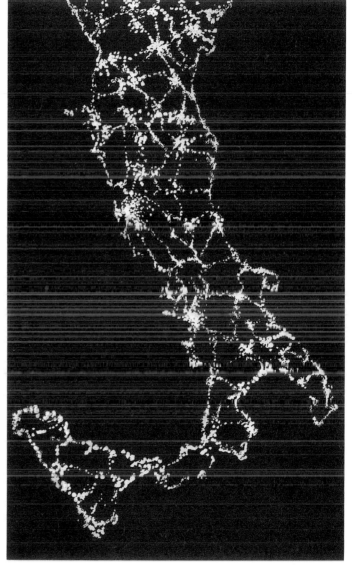

**Make sure that the clusters of white dots are similar in size and shape to the original towns and cities shown on the base map. Leave the sea black.**

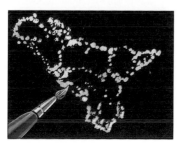

The picture above shows both Sicily and Italy, as they would look at night, from a space satellite. In some areas, such as large towns and cities, the dots are so close together that they merge into blobs of paint. On the outskirts, the dots are more widely spaced. Towns and cities on the coast help to define the shape of the country.

# Old style maps

Pirates drew treasure maps to remind themselves where they had hidden their treasure when they returned to collect it, years later. On some maps, like the one below, the spot where the treasure was hidden was indicated by a coded riddle. The riddle was meant to make the treasure difficult to find if the map fell into the wrong hands.

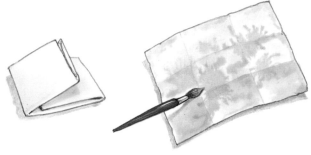

To make an old-looking map, start by folding a sheet of thick watercolour paper several times until it is a small square. Make the creases firm.

Unfold the paper and paint it in a blotchy style with strong, cold tea. You could either use a paintbrush, or wipe a tea bag over the paper.

Let the paper dry. It does not matter if it wrinkles slightly. You could blot some parts with a tissue, to make them look more faded than other parts.

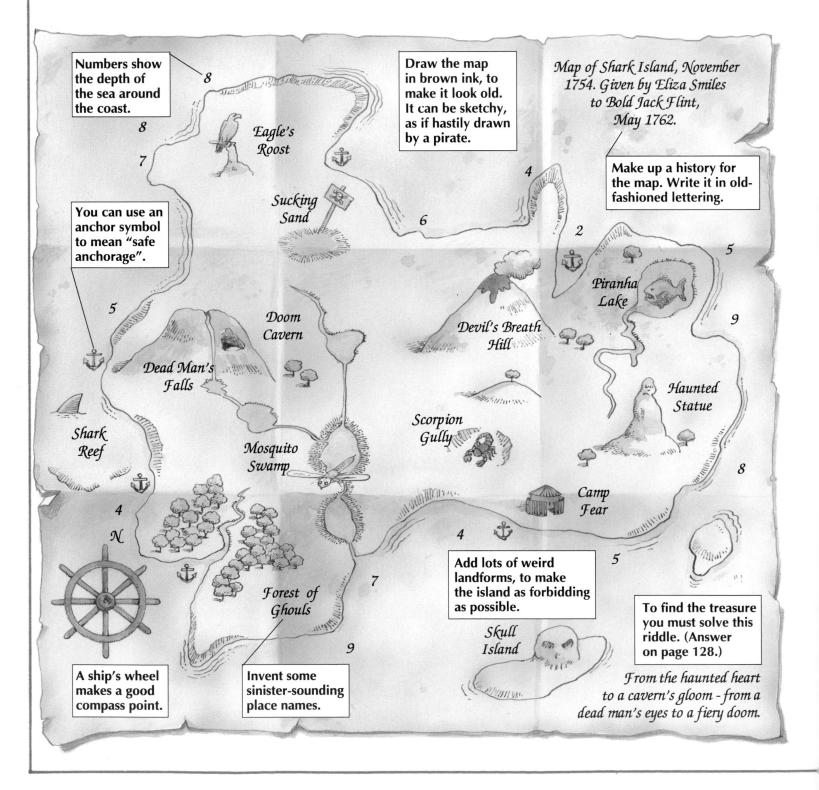

**Numbers show the depth of the sea around the coast.**

**Draw the map in brown ink, to make it look old. It can be sketchy, as if hastily drawn by a pirate.**

*Map of Shark Island, November 1754. Given by Eliza Smiles to Bold Jack Flint, May 1762.*

**Make up a history for the map. Write it in old-fashioned lettering.**

**You can use an anchor symbol to mean "safe anchorage".**

*Eagle's Roost*

*Sucking Sand*

*Doom Cavern*

*Dead Man's Falls*

*Devil's Breath Hill*

*Piranha Lake*

*Haunted Statue*

*Shark Reef*

*Mosquito Swamp*

*Scorpion Gully*

*Camp Fear*

**A ship's wheel makes a good compass point.**

N

*Forest of Ghouls*

**Invent some sinister-sounding place names.**

**Add lots of weird landforms, to make the island as forbidding as possible.**

*Skull Island*

**To find the treasure you must solve this riddle. (Answer on page 128.)**

*From the haunted heart to a cavern's gloom – from a dead man's eyes to a fiery doom.*

# An ancient town map

The map on the right was drawn nearly 350 years ago. It shows a small town called New Amsterdam, which was renamed New York soon after the map was made. It is now the biggest city in the USA.

On the map, the town ends at a wall, which was built to protect citizens from attack. A street called Wall Street now stands on the site of this wall.

The map shows things such as buildings and ships. The effect is a cross between a map and a drawing of the sights you would have seen around the town at that time.

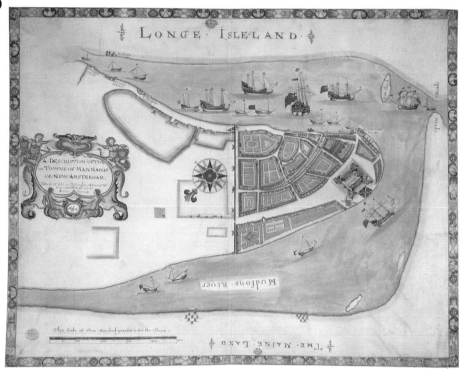

# Drawing an old style town map

To make an old style map of a town that you know, use a base map of the town as it is today. Trace the busiest streets in the middle of the town, including ancient districts. Then trace the map on a fresh piece of paper,

drawing the roads so that the lines look shaky and uneven, like on old maps. Make the buildings look flat and haphazard. Use watercolours in an uneven painting style to add to the old, faded look.

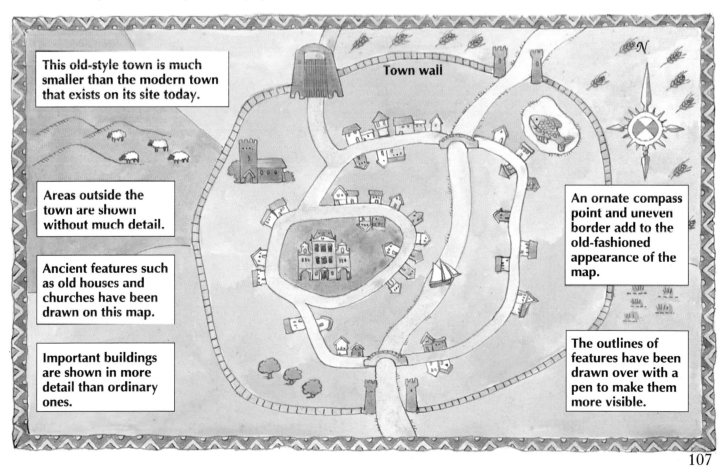

This old-style town is much smaller than the modern town that exists on its site today.

Areas outside the town are shown without much detail.

Ancient features such as old houses and churches have been drawn on this map.

Important buildings are shown in more detail than ordinary ones.

Town wall

An ornate compass point and uneven border add to the old-fashioned appearance of the map.

The outlines of features have been drawn over with a pen to make them more visible.

# A fantasy map

It can be fun to invent a fantasy map full of odd mythical creatures such as trolls and sea-serpents, and hazards such as bottomless marshes and rocky coastlines. An element of mystery can be added to the map by writing its place names in code. You could use the map shown here as inspiration for your own version or you could draw one based on an existing fantasy story.

Before you draw your map, plan some features to show on it. Include elements that will add to the overall atmosphere of the finished picture. You could start by making the paper look old, following the technique shown on page 106.

After you have sketched the map, paint it using watercolours. Use different types of shading to indicate whether an area is safe or not. For example, use warm, light shades to indicate friendly areas. Cold, dingy shades are good for showing hostile areas.

## Coded alphabet

Each rune-like letter shown below corresponds to a letter of the alphabet. Try figuring out the place names on this map, and invent new names to go on your map.

A B C D E F G H I J K L M N O P Q R S T U V W X Y Z

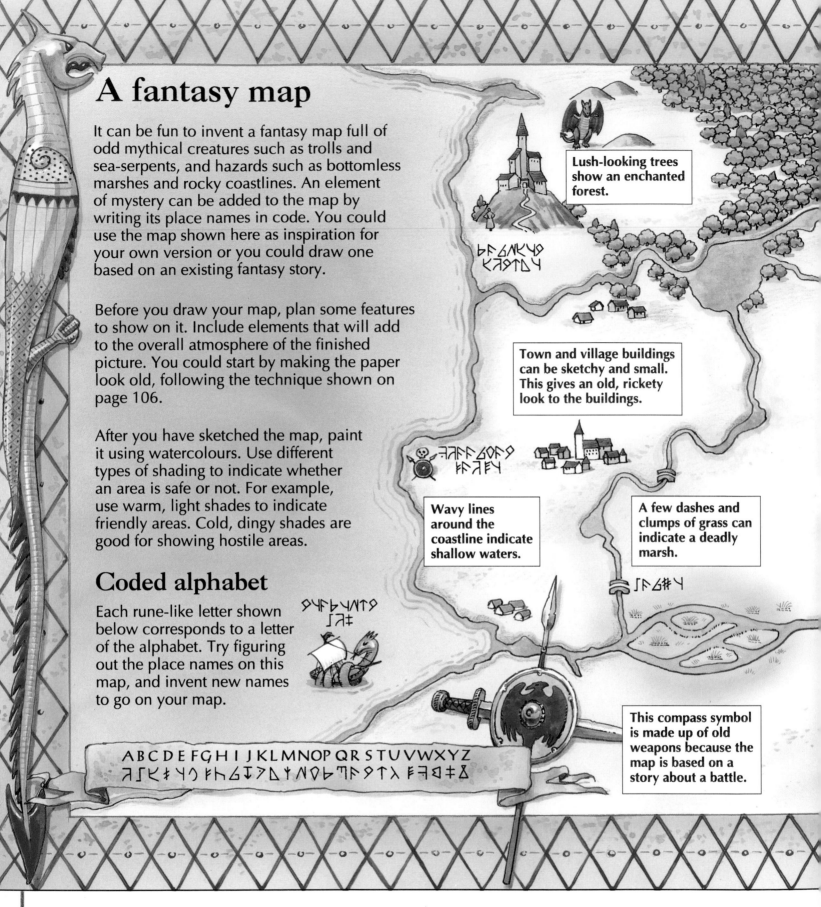

Lush-looking trees show an enchanted forest.

Town and village buildings can be sketchy and small. This gives an old, rickety look to the buildings.

Wavy lines around the coastline indicate shallow waters.

A few dashes and clumps of grass can indicate a deadly marsh.

This compass symbol is made up of old weapons because the map is based on a story about a battle.

## Border designs

You could create a decorative border for your map, more intricate than the one above. Sketch the shapes in pencil, then go over them in pen. You could use gold or silver ink to make the map look precious. Draw the lines freehand so that they are wobbly, making the map look old.

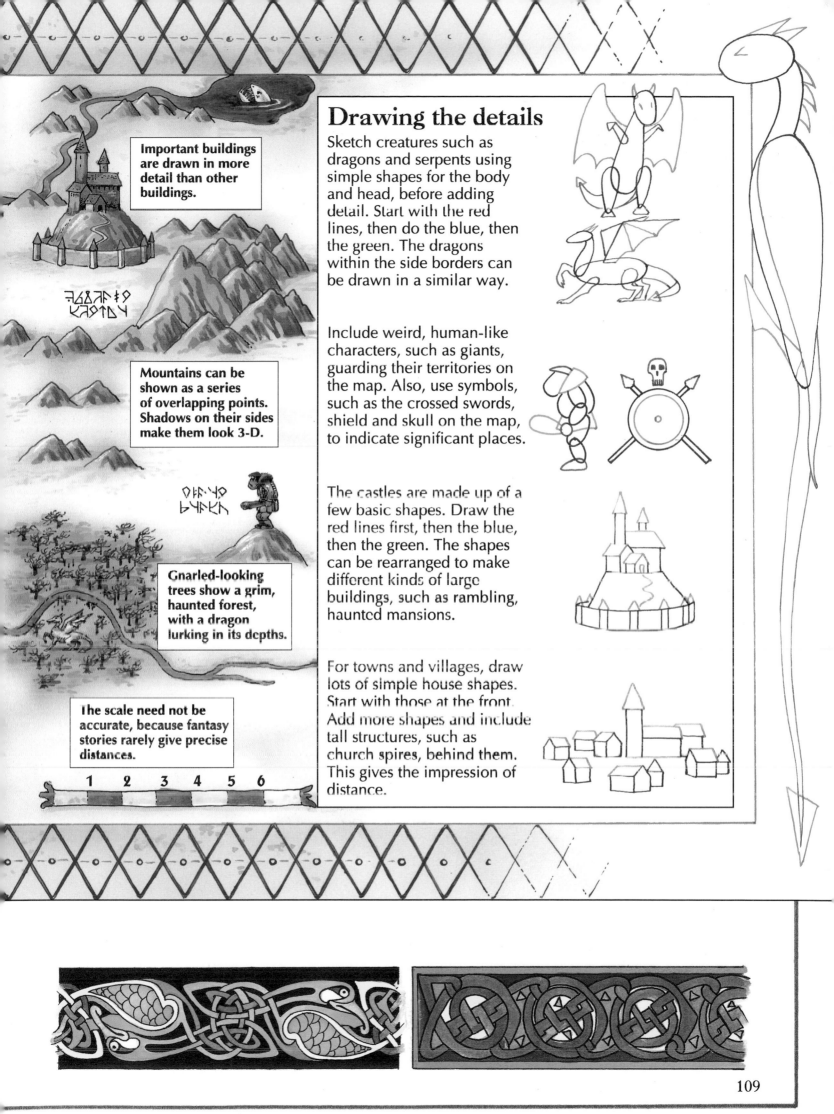

**Important buildings are drawn in more detail than other buildings.**

**Mountains can be shown as a series of overlapping points. Shadows on their sides make them look 3-D.**

**Gnarled-looking trees show a grim, haunted forest, with a dragon lurking in its depths.**

**The scale need not be accurate, because fantasy stories rarely give precise distances.**

1  2  3  4  5  6

# Drawing the details

Sketch creatures such as dragons and serpents using simple shapes for the body and head, before adding detail. Start with the red lines, then do the blue, then the green. The dragons within the side borders can be drawn in a similar way.

Include weird, human-like characters, such as giants, guarding their territories on the map. Also, use symbols, such as the crossed swords, shield and skull on the map, to indicate significant places.

The castles are made up of a few basic shapes. Draw the red lines first, then the blue, then the green. The shapes can be rearranged to make different kinds of large buildings, such as rambling, haunted mansions.

For towns and villages, draw lots of simple house shapes. Start with those at the front. Add more shapes and include tall structures, such as church spires, behind them. This gives the impression of distance.

# Haunted castle game

Floor plans show the layout of the inside of a building. They can be used as the basis for a game, such as the one shown here. This plan shows a haunted castle with secret passages. In the game, characters race around the castle to collect objects. You could invent your own floor plan and game, or trace this plan, enlarge it on a photocopier and decorate it. Name the characters, such as Black Princess and Red Magician, and invent objects to find.

## Playing the game

Put an object in each room except the Dungeon. Throw a dice to move. If you land on a yellow door, you can enter the room to pick up the object. You can go in one door and out through another. You can move to any room if you land on a red trap door, but in return, you must throw the dice to take a risk (see right). When all the other objects have been picked up, race to the Treasure Chest. The game ends when this is collected. The best score wins.

**Draw the pieces with felt tips on paper and cut them out.**

Colour code the pieces to show their values: pink = 4, yellow = 2.

Put the Treasure Chest in the Turret Room. It is worth six points.

**Risks**

| | |
|---|---|
| Send a player back to Start. | ⚀ |
| Spook locks you in. Miss a turn. | ⚁ |
| Ghost gives you the Goblet. | ⚂ |
| Drop one of your objects. | ⚃ |
| Go to Kitchens for a snack. | ⚄ |
| Get chained up in Dungeon. Miss two turns. | ⚅ |

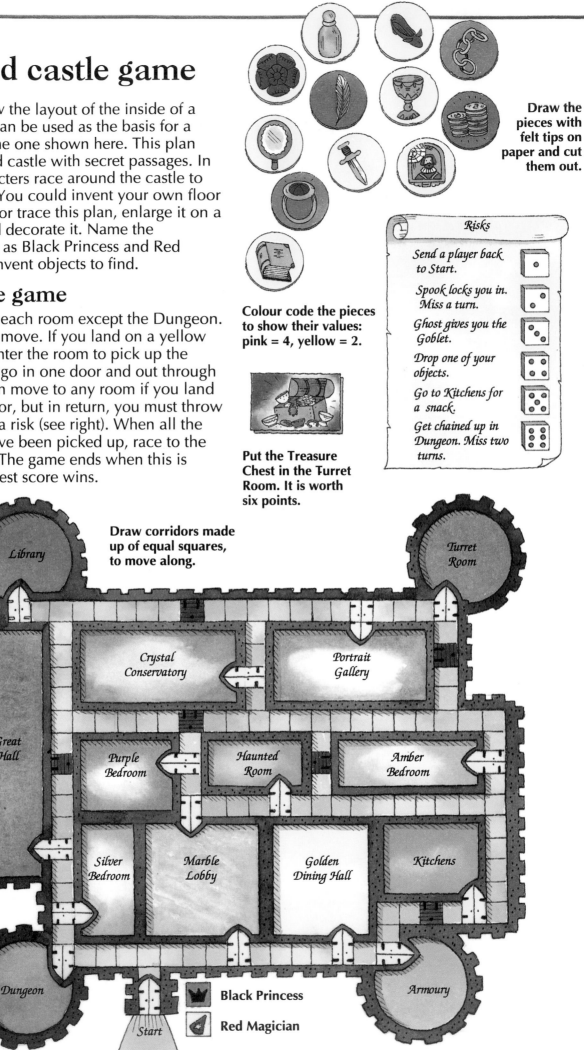

**Draw corridors made up of equal squares, to move along.**

Library

Turret Room

Crystal Conservatory

Portrait Gallery

Great Hall

Purple Bedroom

Haunted Room

Amber Bedroom

Silver Bedroom

Marble Lobby

Golden Dining Hall

Kitchens

Dungeon

Armoury

Start

♛ Black Princess

◤ Red Magician

110

# LETTERING

Many pictures need lettering on them. Maps and comic strips are obvious examples. This next section should help you choose and develop styles suitable for your particular pictures. There are examples of lettering for pictures with different atmospheres, and a number of alphabets in various styles to copy or adapt.

Some methods of drawing and colouring letters can make them into attractive pictures in their own right. There are suggestions in this section for how to use the shapes of letters and how to decorate them in this way.

# Creative lettering

For long passages of text, such as in books, lettering should be as easy to read as possible. However, for shorter messages, such as on posters or invitations, you can use more eye-catching letters. Depending on the effect you want to create, the lettering can suit the message, or it can be in a completely unexpected style. Three examples are shown on the right.

**Forward-slanting writing (called italics) emphasizes the urgency of this message.**

**Letters drawn to make a heart shape suit this romantic message.**

**A message of love in the form of a ransom note would be shocking, but eye-catching and memorable.**

## Making your own lettering

You can keep letters level and even by drawing faint pencil rules, or guidelines. Unless you want very thin or very fat letters, the distance between the guidelines should be between three and nine times the thickest part of your letter.

**Three times the thickest part of the letter.**

**Nine times the thickest part of the letter.**

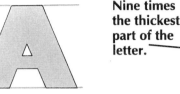

You can also draw a guideline to position the strokes across the middle of some letters. Moving this guideline up or down changes the look of the letters, as shown.

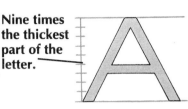

## Small letters

Small letters are just over half as tall as capitals. Small letter sticks (ascenders) and tails (descenders) extend above and below the guidelines by about the same amount. You can vary this for different effects, though.

**Ascender**

**Descender**

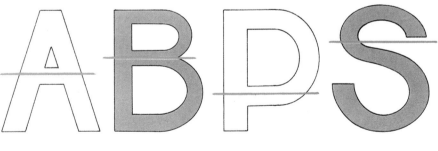

**By using a single guideline through the middle of the letters, you can make them look less rigid.**

**Leave the space of a capital 'E' between words made up of capital letters.**

**Leave the space of a small 'n' between words made up of small letters.**

# Historical lettering

You can give letters a historical feel by copying the different styles that people have used through the ages, such as the Gothic script shown here. This style is effective when used on spooky pictures. It is frequently used for the titles of horror movies.

**The letters are squarish and angular. Small letters are made up of straight lines.**

**You could make this style less creepy-looking by filling in the shapes of the letters using bright felt tips.**

## In a creepy castle

In the Middle Ages, monks wrote books by hand. They often decorated the first letter of a page or paragraph, using beautiful colours. Letters of this type (called illuminated letters) make excellent pictures in their own right.

**Sketch the letter outline first, using pencil.**

**Then decorate the letter in any way you like.**

**Your decoration could illustrate details from a story.**

# Alternative decorations

Here are some other letters, drawn in various styles and decorated to create particular atmospheres. You could make entire alphabets decorated in these styles, or even invent alphabets of your own, to provide titles for drawings that you have done.

**Hot. Red, orange and yellow are warm colours.**

**Cold. Icy blues and greens are cold colours.**

**Natural. The letter looks as if it is alive and growing.**

**Marine. The outline ripples, like water.**

**Horrific. The letter looks like a slab of stone, similar to a grave stone.**

# Comic strip lettering

In comic strips, lettering must be easy to read, but it has several jobs to do. For example, it shows what people say or think in bubbles. Also, it provides sound effects and contributes to the sense of drama, so it should be drawn in a variety of sizes and different shapes.

## Sound effects

When you create a sound effect, to get an idea of which letters to use, imagine what the sound would look like if it was shown as a word. There are examples here and in the story below.

You can make the sound effect stand out by drawing shapes around the words.

Match the size of the lettering with the loudness of the sound effect.

You can even draw little pictures to add emphasis to the sound effect.

## Speech bubbles

For speech, it is best to do the lettering before you draw the bubble outline. Use a pen with a fine tip to draw the letters.

To ensure that the letters will be the same height, draw parallel pencil rules and write the letters in between them, as shown here. Then erase the pencil lines, so that the speech looks neat.

A speech bubble can show how words are said. For instance, huge letters in a jagged bubble make words look loud.

# "Graffiti" styles

Graffiti styles look bold and vivid. The styles developed when people began spraying their names on subway trains and walls in New York in the 1960s. It is illegal to write graffiti on walls but you can use the style on paper.

Good graffiti needs careful planning, so sketch your idea in rough before doing the real thing. For a quick guide, see how the piece on the right is put together.

**Add a firm outline around the letters and around the whole piece.**

**The letters are blocked out roughly, using the chosen lettering style.**

**A background, scenery and decoration are added. These help to enliven the letters.**

**The colours are worked out and applied. Bold colours ensure that the effect is eye-catching.**

## Tags

A tag is a graffiti writer's signature. It is usually a nickname. You could design a tag and use it instead of signing your name. It should be striking and easy to recognize.

On walls, graffiti art is usually made using spray paints. On paper, you can copy the effect using marker pens. The wider the tip, the quicker you can colour your graffiti.

**The quickest sort of tag to write is one colour only. This sort is called a throw-up. It has an outline around letters in a single colour.**

## "Wildstyle" graffiti

This complex design has a pattern of interlocking letters which can be quite difficult to read. It is called wildstyle.

**You could add some brilliant sparkles to some of the letters.**

**You could incorporate images that are associated with your subject (such as jet planes and skyscrapers for New York) into your graffiti. Also, you could replace a letter with a cartoon character.**

# Alphabets to copy

Here are some alphabets to trace or copy, to incorporate in pictures and designs. The first might be useful for messages that need to be clear, unfussy and easy to read.

# ABCDEFGHIJKLM
# NOPQRSTUVWXYZ
## abcdefghijklmnopqrst
## uvwxyz 1234567890

## Gothic

Here is a complete alphabet of Gothic style lettering, similar to the examples shown on page 113. To give letters like these a precious look you could decorate them using gold and silver ink.

# ABCDEFGHIJKLM
# NOPQRSTUVWXYZ
## abcdefghijklmnopqrstuvwxyz
# 1234567890

## Italic

Before printing was invented, hand drawn italic lettering was sometimes used to write whole books. The style is still popular with calligraphers* today.

*ABCDEFGHIJKLM
NOPQRSTUVWXYZ
abcdefghijklmnopqrstuv
wxyz 1234567890*

## Art Nouveau

This typeface was designed to complement an artistic style called Art Nouveau. Its curved, natural-looking shapes are effective when it is designed decoratively into a picture.

ABCDEFGHIJKLM
NOPQRSTUVWXYZ
abcdefghijklmnopqrstuv
wxyz 1234567890

---

*A calligrapher is somebody who draws decorative lettering by hand.

## Comic lettering style

This typeface is designed to look like lettering that has been hand written. It is clear but slightly uneven. You could base your hand lettering on it, for use in a comic strip.

ABCDEFGHIJKL
MNOPQRSTUV
WXYZ abcdefghij
klmnopqrstuvwxyz
1234567890

## Outlined lettering

This bold typeface would suit a loud-looking poster. Copy the outline shapes first, with an ink pen, then fill in the middles, using a thick marker pen.

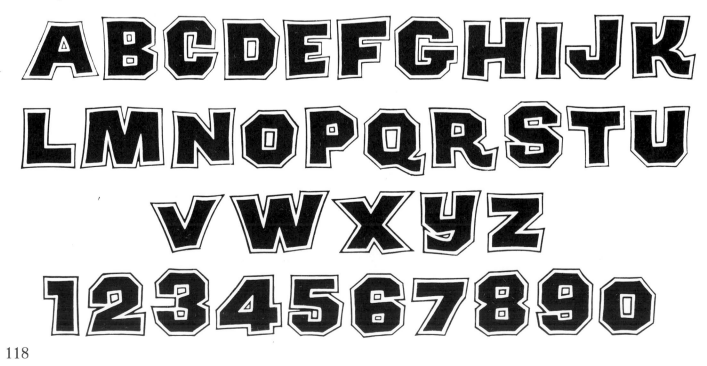

ABCDEFGHIJK
LMNOPQRSTU
VWXYZ
1234567890

# TECHNIQUES AND MATERIALS

The final section of this book is a reference section which contains general information about drawing and colouring.

The techniques of drawing in perspective, and how to take account of foreshortening, are explained. There is a round-up of materials and tools which you might like to experiment with, and plenty of advice about what is on sale so that you don't feel bewildered when confronted by a baffling display of goods in an art shop.

The glossary on pages 126-127 explains terms connected with drawing so that you will be able to read other books without being confused by jargon.

# Perspective

Drawing scenes in perspective means drawing them the way your eyes see them, so that objects look smaller the further away they are. Scenes such as the one on the right can be constructed using imaginary points, called vanishing points, and guide lines drawn to the vanishing points, called disappearing lines.

A vanishing point is the point where parallel lines would appear to meet if they were continued winto the distance from where they are seen.

When sketching a perspective picture, the position of the horizon should be chosen and sketched first, with the vanishing point on it, as shown in stage 1.

Next, the features that are in perspective should be sketched, as shown in stage 2, using disappearing lines to help plot them in their correct positions.

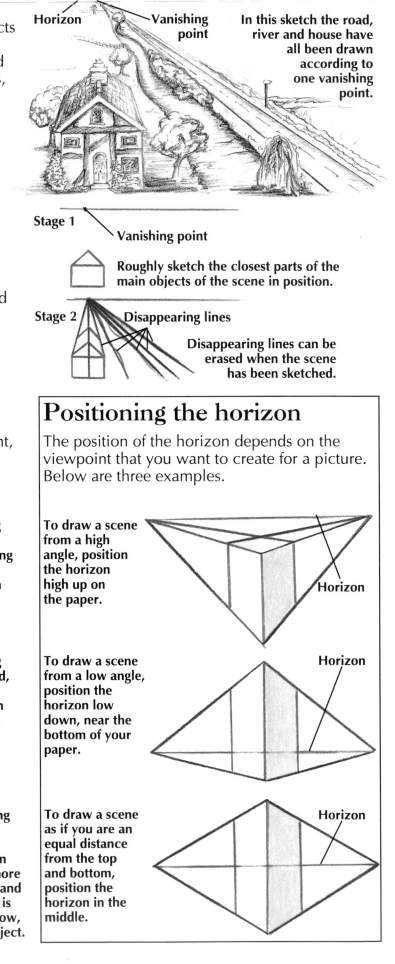

**Horizon** · **Vanishing point**

In this sketch the road, river and house have all been drawn according to one vanishing point.

**Stage 1** · **Vanishing point**

Roughly sketch the closest parts of the main objects of the scene in position.

**Stage 2** · **Disappearing lines**

Disappearing lines can be erased when the scene has been sketched.

## Vanishing points

Scenes can have more than one vanishing point, according to where the picture is seen from, called its viewpoint.

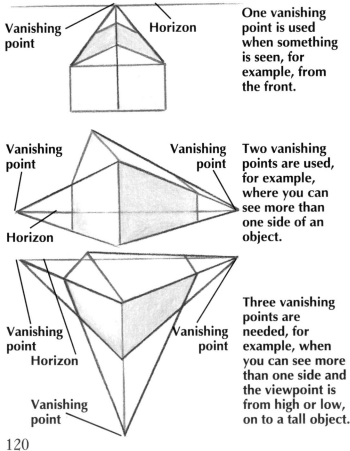

**Vanishing point** / **Horizon**

One vanishing point is used when something is seen, for example, from the front.

**Vanishing point** / **Vanishing point** / **Horizon**

Two vanishing points are used, for example, where you can see more than one side of an object.

**Vanishing point** / **Horizon** / **Vanishing point** / **Vanishing point**

Three vanishing points are needed, for example, when you can see more than one side and the viewpoint is from high or low, on to a tall object.

## Positioning the horizon

The position of the horizon depends on the viewpoint that you want to create for a picture. Below are three examples.

To draw a scene from a high angle, position the horizon high up on the paper.

**Horizon**

To draw a scene from a low angle, position the horizon low down, near the bottom of your paper.

**Horizon**

To draw a scene as if you are an equal distance from the top and bottom, position the horizon in the middle.

**Horizon**

120

# A scene in detail

This scene shows ways in which an impression of distance can be given to a picture.

**Repeated objects, such as the trees in this picture, reinforce the sense of perspective.**

**People and objects in the foreground are drawn in more detail than in the background. Also, in a realistic scene, the colours can be faded slightly towards the background.**

**Figures are connected by putting some partly in front of others. This technique helps to lead the viewer's eye into the picture.**

# People in perspective

Vanishing point

When showing people in a line, directly behind each other, the closest person should be sketched first. Draw disappearing lines from the person's feet and head to the nearest vanishing point. Show the people behind inside these lines.

For people not directly behind one another, sketch an upright line inside the disappearing lines, level with where you want another person to go. Draw horizontal lines across from this, where the lines meet, then draw the person inside these lines.

# Foreshortening

Foreshortening describes the fact that when things are drawn in perspective, parts that are coming towards you appear shorter than they really are. As an example, notice how, as this person's arm raises, the distance between the raised hand and the body looks squashed.

Drawing pictures of foreshortened things is tricky. Give yourself practice by sketching long objects, such as bottles, from a variety of angles.

**The hand appears to get bigger because it gets closer to you.**

# Artists' materials

Pencils should form the basis of your drawing kit. They are cheap and are available with a variety of leads, from very hard (9H) to very soft (9B).

Soft leads, from 9B to B, give dark lines and are useful for dark shading. B stands for black. The higher the number, the softer and more smudgy the lead.

Hard leads, from 9H to H, are useful for creating precise lines and light shading. H stands for hard. The higher the number, the harder the lead.

## Coloured pencils

You can create different effects with coloured pencils. For example, by varying the pressure on the pencil you can vary its tone. By pressing harder you can make the colour appear stronger. This technique can be combined with all other colour pencil effects, such as those shown on the right.

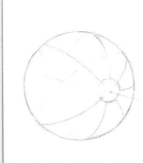

This sketch was done with a medium hard pencil (2H). It has marked the paper well, but is not so soft that it will smudge before the drawing is complete.

The sketch for this picture was done with a very hard pencil (9H), which scored the paper. Thin white lines show through the shaded picture.

**Light pressure**  **Heavy pressure**

Hatching. The strength of a colour can be varied by altering the space between the strokes.

Cross hatching. More pencil strokes are used than for hatching, so the tones are stronger.

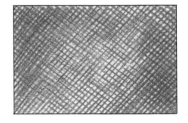

Hatching two or more colours together can create a new colour. This is most effective from a distance.

Colours can be mixed by dotting them close together. The effect is called stippling.

Some coloured pencils are water soluble. If you paint a wash of water over them, they give a result that looks similar to watercolour.

## Charcoal and chalk

Charcoal and chalk both mark paper easily, so they are ideal for creating bold, loose sketches and effects.

Both charcoal and chalk tend to smudge. Use a spray-on fixative as soon as you have finished the picture. This is available from art shops.

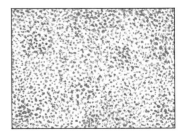

Charcoal can be smudged with your finger tip to make lines look less harsh and create soft shadows.

Chalk is useful for adding highlights on top of dark colours.

Use the end of the chalk to create crisp highlights. The side can be used to create softer, more subtle highlights.

# Felt tips and markers

Felt tips and markers tend to give strong tones. They are well suited to pictures that must leave a strong impression, such as on information posters, or comic style drawings.

Like felt tips, marker pens are available with a variety of thicknesses of tips, and some use water based inks. However, other types use spirit based inks. The spirit based inks do not smudge if one colour is put on top of another.

Usually, felt tips contain water based inks, which smudge when they touch.

This patch shows that when one colour is put on top of another, a new colour is formed.

Felt tips are available with a variety of tips. The finer the tips, the closer the details that you can show in your pictures.

A broad tipped marker (below) is ideal for creating large areas of colour.

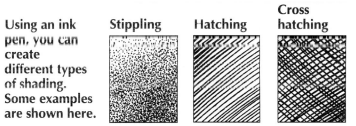

# Ink pens

Ink pens are useful for creating outlines and shadows. They can look effective when used with a variety of different colouring materials, including watercolours, inks and felt tips. The best quality pens are called technical pens, but they are expensive. Cheaper, plastic tipped pens are available, which also make very fine lines.

Using an ink pen, you can create different types of shading. Some examples are shown here.

| Stippling | Hatching | Cross hatching |
|---|---|---|

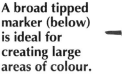

# Airbrushes

Airbrushes use compressed air to blow paint onto a surface. They can produce fine lines, soft tones and solid areas of colour. They are complicated tools, which cost a lot of money to buy. Artists' airbrushes are the most expensive, but cheaper versions, called modellers' airbrushes, are also available.

Different effects can be created depending on how far, and at what angle, the airbrush is held from the paper.

Pressing this lever controls the air flow. Pulling it back controls the paint supply.

The airbrush is held at between 45° and 80° to the paper.

80°  45°

# Airbrush effects

For fine lines, the airbrush is held close to the paper. The button is pulled back slightly, to allow a small amount of paint through the nozzle.

To make even colour, the airbrush is held 10cm (4in) from the paper and even strokes are made. Each new stroke overlaps the previous one.

For graduated tone, the amount of paint that is blown onto the paper (and therefore its tone) is increased with each new stroke of the airbrush.

To make graduated colours, the colour of the paint is altered slightly after each stroke of the airbrush. The result is a subtle blend of different colours.

# Paints and inks

Watercolours are available in tubes, bottles and dried blocks. You can control the strength of colour, depending on how much water you use when you mix them.

**A tube of watercolour.**

**The tones on the right have been made by mixing dark green with water, in different proportions.**

100% watercolour (from a tube)

25% water  75% watercolour

50% water  50% watercolour

75% water  25% watercolour

Gouache is available in tubes. It gives more solid tones than watercolours. With gouache, you can correct mistakes by painting over them.

Poster paints are cheaper than gouache, but the quality and choice of colours is not so good.

**Gouache is good for creating solid areas of colour.**

**This patch shows that unlike watercolour, with gouache or poster paints you can apply dark colours first, then paint over them with lighter colours.**

Inks give bright, vibrant colours. They can be applied with a brush, by pen or by airbrush. You can dilute their colours, to give pale effects that look like watercolours.

**Coloured inks are usually supplied in pots.**

**The tones on the right have been created by mixing a water based ink with various amounts of water.**

100% ink

75% ink  25% water

50% ink  50% water

25% ink  75% water

# Paint colours

The patches on the right show a good selection of artist's colours. A range like this will enable you to create almost any colour you need by mixing them in different quantities.

| | | |
|---|---|---|
| White | Crimson | |
| Cadmium yellow | Ultramarine blue | |
| Yellow ochre | Indian red | |
| Cadmium red | Cobalt blue | |
| Raw umber | Viridian | |
| Burnt sienna | Ivory black | |

Here are some examples of the colours that you can make by mixing different colours.

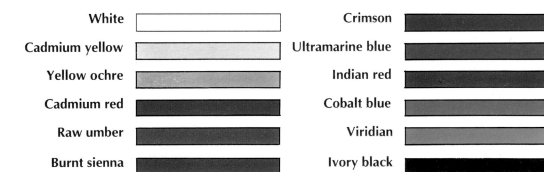

# Brushes

Brushes are made either from animal hair, or from synthetic materials such as nylon. They come in a range of sizes (numbered from one, the smallest, to twelve, the largest) and are available with different types of ends. Some examples are shown here, along with some of their various effects. For watercolours, use soft brushes. For thicker paints, such as gouache, you can use coarser brushes.

**Round. These are most useful for producing fine details.**

**Chisel end. Used to paint pictures with precise edges.**

**Filbert. Their flat ends make them good for creating shaped, tapering marks.**

**A number one size brush. This is used for tiny details.**

**A number twelve size. Used for painting large areas quickly.**

**You can buy a stippling brush or make one by cutting the end off an old brush.**

# Paper

Rough sketch paper is ideal for sketching. However, it is not strong enough to have colours put on it. When painted on, it tends to wrinkle. Felt tips and markers smudge when used on sketch paper, as shown above right.

Smooth, plain paper is adequate for most drawings. It is ideal for colour pencils, but because it is thin, it tends to wrinkle when watery paint is put on it.

Cold pressed paper has a slightly rough surface. It is ideal for watercolours and gouache.

Charcoal looks striking on cold pressed paper (right), because it shows the grains of the paper.

## Weights of paper

Papers' weights are given in grams per square metre (gsm) or pounds (lb). The heavier the paper, the more expensive it will be. Heavier papers are less likely to wrinkle than thin papers.

# Stretching paper

To prevent thinner papers from wrinkling when you use paints, stretch them before you begin painting. To stretch the paper, you need a board, some gummed tape, a sponge and water. Generally, papers below 400gsm (200lb) should be stretched before you paint on them.

**Wet, but do not soak, the paper thoroughly with a wet sponge. Secure one side of the paper to the board, using gummed tape.**

**Working clockwise, tape the edges with the gummed tape. Wrinkles on the paper should smooth out when dry.**

**Leave the paper on the board while you do your painting. When it has dried, cut it out with a sharp knife.**

# Glossary

**Abstract art** A work of art that is a pattern of colours and shapes, rather than a picture of something recognizable.

**Acrylic paints** Paints made from coloured **pigment** mixed with a chemical binder. Used by themselves, these paints dry quickly. They can be mixed with a chemical to slow down the rate of drying, so that they behave like **oil paints**.

**Airbrush** A tool for spraying paint onto a surface by means of compressed air. The airbrush itself looks like a fat pen. It is connected by a long flexible tube to an air compressor, which blows air through the airbrush, spraying a mist of paint onto the surface that is being painted.

**Calligraphy** The art of creating lettering by hand. It is usually designed to be decorative and pleasing to look at.

**Canvas** A surface made from woven material, for painting on, especially when using **acrylic** or **oil paints**. Canvas made from pure linen is the best quality, but good quality cotton and linen-cotton mixes are cheaper and make good substitutes. Before it is painted on, canvas is usually stretched and fixed to a frame called a stretcher, which makes it tight and slightly springy.

**Caricature** A drawing in which a person's features are exaggerated to create a funny, **cartoon**-like picture.

**Cartoon** Today, this is the name given to a simple picture, usually funny looking, which can be drawn in a variety of styles. A series of cartoon pictures, often with speech and sound effects added, is called a cartoon strip.

Traditionally, a cartoon was the name given to a full-sized drawing on paper, which was used as a design for artwork such as paintings, tapestries or mosaics.

**Cartouche** A decorated panel, often in the shape of a scroll, used especially on antique maps, containing written information such as the map's title, or the scale (or both).

**Charcoal** A drawing material made by partly burning pieces of wood, usually willow or vine twigs. Pure charcoal is black, soft and dusty, and smudges easily. It is supplied in sticks. Compressed charcoal is a mixture of charcoal and a binding medium, to make it harder than pure charcoal. This is available in sticks and also in pencils.

**Coloured pencils** Pencils with centres made from a mixture of coloured **pigment**, clay and a binding medium. They are available in a wide variety of different colours.

**Composition** The way that subjects are arranged when they are drawn, so that the finished picture appears to have an order, and does not just look like a disorganized collection of things.

**Disappearing lines** Guidelines that are used when drawing objects in **perspective**. They are drawn from the nearest points of an object towards the **vanishing points**.

**Easel** An upright frame that holds a **canvas** (or other surface) while it is painted on. A type of easel called a radial easel is the most useful, as it is light and can be folded up and carried around easily.

**Figurative art** A work of art that shows recognizable objects, but not necessarily in a realistic way.

**Foreshortening** The apparent shortening of an object when it is seen from a particular **viewpoint**. For example, when a person is viewed from above, the distance between the head and the lower parts appears shorter than it really is.

**Gouache** Paints made from coloured **pigment** mixed with gum, with white pigment added to them to make them opaque (not see-through). They can be used thickly, like **oil paints**, or diluted and used almost like **watercolours**.

**Highlight** The appearance of light on part of an object, caused by light bouncing off it. Artists often show the highlights, as well as **shadows**, that form on a thing in order to emphasize its solidity and shape.

**Mask** A piece of paper or clear sticky-backed plastic, cut to a specific shape, which is used to block off, or mask, part of a picture to prevent paint from getting on it while another part is being painted. Masking fluid is also available, which can be painted on to the picture and rubbed off. Masks are usually needed when pictures are painted using an **airbrush**.

**Mid-tone** An area of a picture that can be described as neither **highlight** nor **shadow**.

**Neatline** A border around a map. Usually these are white, but they are sometimes highly decorated, particularly on antique maps.

**Oil paints** Paints made from coloured **pigment** mixed with oil. They are sticky and slow to dry. They can be used thick or, mixed with a chemical such as turpentine or white spirit, in thin washes. Mistakes can be corrected easily by scraping off or wiping off the bad area and painting over it again.

**Palette**  A smooth surface on which paint is mixed. (This word can also be used to describe the range of colours that an artist selects to use in a picture.)

**Pastels**  Sticks of soft, pure coloured **pigment** held together loosely with binding gum. They tend to be crumbly, which can make them difficult to work with.

**Perspective**  The technique of drawing objects and scenes so that the correct impressions of distance, size and detail are given.

**Pigment**  Coloured minerals or chemicals, either natural or man made, that are used to provide the colour in artists' drawing and painting materials. As an example, to make the middle for a pure red **coloured pencil**, pure red pigment is mixed with clay and a binding medium.

**Pointillism**  A French word describing a shading technique where dots of pure colour are put onto a picture, by **stippling**, to show colours and shadows. When viewed from a distance, the dots appear to blend and form different colours and textures.

**Portrait**  A detailed drawing of a real person or animal, especially the face. Often, portraits are realistic, but they can be unrealistic, so long as they show the nature of the subject.

**Poster paints**  Cheaper types of **gouache**, made using lower quality **pigment** and gum.

**Primary colours**  The three basic colours: red, blue and yellow. These can be mixed together to make other colours, but cannot be made by mixing other colours.

**Proportions**  The size of one thing compared to another. In a realistic drawing or painting, things that are in proportion must have the same proportions as the real things that they represent.

**Realism**  A style of drawing where the artist tries to show scenes and subjects as realistically as possible.

**Scumbling**  The technique of applying paint with a nearly dry brush using a scrubbing motion. The technique is used for blending hard outlines or for breaking up a layer of colour so that another layer underneath shows through, creating a soft effect.

**Secondary colours**  The three colours that can be made by mixing together equal amounts of two **primary colours**. The colours that can be created are orange (a mixture of red and yellow), green (blue and yellow) and purple (red and blue).

**Shadow**  An area on something that is shaded from the light, so that it appears dark.

**Still life**  A drawing or painting of non-moving objects, such as fruit or flowers. A still life can be useful practice, because the artist has time to study the subject without it changing or moving.

**Stippling**  Drawing or painting with dots instead of lines or patches of colour. Stippling can be made with any kind of artist's material, such as a brush, pencil or felt tip.

**Tone**  The depth of a colour. Different tones of the same colour can be created, depending on how hard a **coloured pencil** is pressed when shading or how diluted a paint is.

**Typeface**  A full set of characters, including letters of the alphabet, numbers and punctuation marks, made to a particular design. Typefaces are used to create the printed letters and words that appear in such things as books, comics, newspapers and posters.

**Vanishing point**  The point at which **disappearing lines** appear to meet on a scene that is drawn in **perspective**.

**Viewpoint**  The apparent position, created by the illustrator, from which a viewer sees the contents of a picture when looking at it. For example, when looking at a picture of a skyscraper that is drawn as if from high above, the viewer sees the picture from a high viewpoint.

**Wash**  A layer of paint applied over an entire area in a picture. If it is the first application of paint, over which extra washes or shadow will be applied, the wash is known as a base wash.

**Watercolours**  Paints made from **pigment** mixed with gum and diluted with water. When mixed, they are more liquid than **oil paints** and have to be applied more thinly. They tend to dry quickly, which can make them difficult to correct if a mistake is made.

# Index

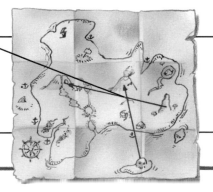

**Solution to treasure map riddle (from page 106)**

Draw a line from the Haunted Statue to Doom Cavern ("From the haunted heart to a cavern's gloom") and another line from the skull on Skull Island to the volcano called Devil's Breath Hill ("from a dead man's eyes to a fiery doom"). Where the lines cross, the treasure is buried, as shown here.

You could write a puzzle for your map. Show it to your friends and let them try to locate the treasure.